As always, in memory of
Francine.

With thanks to my Beta Readers,
particularly to CS for his patient editing and
technical help,
and more especially, for his friendship.

Dedicated to the people of Newbridge, in the
Republic of Ireland, with apologies for my
inadequate representation of their wonderfully
musical speech.

And for my granddaughter, Lyla.

Cover Art: GL Robinson, 2023.

For a FREE short story please go to my website:
https://romancenovelsbyglrobinson.com

or use the code below on your phone:

Repairing a Broken Heart

A Regency Romance

By

GL Robinson

©GL Robinson 2023. All Rights Reserved.

Contents

Prologue 1
Chapter One 5
Chapter Two 9
Chapter Three 15
Chapter Four 21
Chapter Five 27
Chapter Six 33
Chapter Seven 39
Chapter Eight 45
Chapter Nine 51
Chapter Ten 57
Chapter Eleven 61
Chapter Twelve 65
Chapter Thirteen 71
Chapter Fourteen 77
Chapter Fifteen 83
Chapter Sixteen 89
Chapter Seventeen 95
Chapter Eighteen 101
Chapter Nineteen 105
Chapter Twenty 109
Chapter Twenty-One 113
Chapter Twenty-Two 117
Chapter Twenty-Three 123
Chapter Twenty-Four 131
Chapter Twenty-Five 139

Chapter Twenty-Six	145
Chapter Twenty-Seven	149
Chapter Twenty-Eight	153
Chapter Twenty-Nine	157
Chapter Thirty	159
Chapter Thirty-One	161
Chapter Thirty-Two	165
Chapter Thirty-Three	169
Chapter Thirty-Four	173
Chapter Thirty-Five	177
Chapter Thirty-Six	183
Chapter Thirty-Seven	189
Chapter Thirty-Eight	193
Chapter Thirty-Nine	197
Chapter Forty	203
Chapter Forty-One	205
Chapter Forty-Two	209
Chapter Forty-Three	215
Chapter Forty-Four	221
Chapter Forty-Five	225
Chapter Forty-Six	231
A Note from the Author	233
An excerpt from GL Robinson's next novel	235
About The Author	241

Prologue

Middlesex

"No," said Lyla to the gentleman in front of her, "I won't sell you Mercury."

"Why not?" The gentleman scowled. "I'm prepared to meet your price."

"I know you to be a bruising rider with no thought about the welfare of your mount. Then last week when I was in the village doing a few errands I saw your horse, the one you're riding today," she gestured towards a dispirited-looking animal with its head hanging down. "I saw it standing outside the inn in a sharp wind. It was there when I went to the baker's at the other end of the street and still there when I came back some time later. It would only have cost you a farthing or two to have a lad walk it out of the wind. I won't sell my horses to anyone who doesn't know how to look after them."

"It's no business of yours how I treat my horses!"

"No, but it is my business how you treat one of mine. Good day, Sir Laurence. I'm sorry to bring our discussion to an end, but I'm busy."

His lordship watched as the woman walked away from him, tapping her crop against the side of her well-used serge riding dress, apparently oblivious to the straw adhering to the back of it. He knew she couldn't be more than twenty but she had the assurance of a much older woman. His temper rose. Who did she think she was, refusing to sell him a damned horse? He'd always done business with these stables as his father had before him. The

Worsley Stables had been a fixture in these parts for generations and had done well out of all of them, as the fine old house and extensive stables and paddocks testified.

He'd known her all his life. As a girl, she'd always been horse-mad, running in and out of the stables, riding horses far too big for her, her face streaked with dirt, her wild hair all over the place and her petticoat inches deep in mud. She was some five years his junior but showed no more deference to his age than to his rank. She either ignored him or pointed out his shortcomings. She told him he had the worst seat in the county; his stirrups were too long, he was jerking his reins, or when he'd proudly tooled around with his new curricle, she said he'd poled his horses up too tight and didn't know how to point his leaders.

Then he'd been off at Cambridge — damned waste of time except for the good pals he'd met there — and hadn't come back to the family estate for a couple of years. The next time he saw her, he hadn't believed his eyes. It was at the Squire's annual May Ball. There she was, no longer the hoyden in a dirty petticoat but a young lady in a fashionable gown that did nothing to hide her womanly charms. She was looking bored until that chap Harry Blankley approached her. Then he saw that when she smiled, dimples appeared in her heart-shaped face.

When at last she was alone he'd made his way to her side.

"Miss Worsley," he said, making his best bow and favoring her with the meaningful look with which he'd ingratiated himself into more than one maiden's heart, "how nice to see you again."

"Is it?" she'd countered. No smile or dimples appeared on her face. "I'm surprised to hear you say that. We never got on well when we were younger. As I recall, you're a cow-fisted rider but refused any advice to help you improve."

He had been going to ask her to dance, but at that, he'd turned on his heel and left. He wondered furiously why some older female hadn't taken her in hand. Get her to act like a young lady, teach her to sew or whatever it was they did. Above all, teach her to know her place. She'd obviously never learned that.

He regarded her narrowly now, unable, in spite of his anger, to ignore her shapely rear and the trim waist accentuated by the rather threadbare close fitting riding jacket. There'd been some story about her and Blankley, but then she'd disappeared, and Blankley had married that heiress, Daphne Something. He'd heard she'd gone to Ireland but now here she was, back home and paying him as little respect as ever. Well, this was the last time she'd speak to him like that. He was Sir Laurence now, and if no one had ever taught her before, she'd damned well learn who her betters were. He'd bring her to her knees if it was the last thing he did.

Chapter One

Eighteen Months Earlier

"I absolutely refuse to marry Malcom Foxworthy." Lyla confronted her father in the library, whither she had been summoned. "I don't love him. In fact I don't even like him."

Her father would have torn his hair had it not been carefully pomaded to cover an unfortunate thinning over the top.

"Is that all you've got to say?" Anger suffused his face. "I shelled out the blunt for a London season to get you safely settled and you had several advantageous offers, all of which you refused. If you're holding out for young Blankley, let me tell you, you're wasting your time. Now he's back from his travels I hear he's been seeing a lot of Daphne Warner. She's got a good deal more to offer than you have. I daresay she don't know as much about horses as you do, but she has twenty thousand a year. For Blankley Senior that's a good deal more to the purpose than being able to mix a poultice, I can tell you. Everyone's saying they're only just staying ahead of the bailiffs."

He stood in front of the mirror. He was used to being thought a good-looking man and was vain of his appearance. Now his high color showed not only on his face but up in his scalp, barely covered by his thinning hair. That distressed him more than his daughter's intransigence. He took a deep breath and patted his coiffure, trying to regain his composure.

"I blame your mother," he said at last. "If she hadn't upped and died like that, you'd have had someone to get you ready for a man instead of spending all your time in the stables."

"It wasn't poor Mama's fault she contracted a fever! And anyway, I don't think it would have made any difference. I never could learn to sew, or draw, or play the pianoforte. All those governesses tried their best but it was no use. The only thing I'm good at is dealing with horses. And you know that's a good thing, Papa. You've got to admit I'm helpful there."

"That's as may be. But the stables ain't going to help you get a husband, Lyla! You're good-looking, like everyone on my side of the family," he caught sight of himself again in the large gilt mirror over the fireplace and preened, thrusting his shoulders back, "and there's no denying you'd make any man a cozy armful. But no one's going to be looking for you in the stalls with the horses. No one except young Blankley and as I said, he's spoken for. He's marrying Daphne Warner."

"He can't be! Who is Daphne Warner? I know no one by that name! Harry has never mentioned her! He and I have an… an understanding, Papa. He told me his family needs money. He knows Mama didn't leave me very much. Our stables do well, but not enough to give the Blankleys what they need."

"They certainly don't! Anyway, as I said, it all arranged. Whether you know her or not, he's to marry the Warner girl."

"You must be mistaken, Papa, really. He has a plan! He told me he was going to India to take up some business or the other and make enough money to send home. Then in three or four years when he's cleared the debts, he'll come home to marry me. I said I'd wait."

"Three or four years? Are you mad? If the bailiffs are at the gate they don't have three or four weeks!"

"But Harry said…"

"Listen to me, my girl. I don't care what Harry said. He'll do his duty by his family and if it means marrying the Warner girl, that's what he'll do."

"I don't believe it!" Lyla brushed angry tears from her eyes. "I'm going there right now to ask him myself."

It was a testimony to his daughter's independent ways that her father found nothing remarkable in this announcement. He was used to her going off where and when she liked. He never worried that she might get into trouble and barely remembered the one time when she had. She was about twelve and hadn't come back by dinner time. He might not have noticed that either, had her maid Potter not come to him, worried that Miss Lyla hadn't come home and it was getting dark. He'd been persuaded to send out a search party and they'd found her lying in a ditch with her horse next to her.

"It wasn't Bobby's fault," she said, "He didn't see the dip and neither did I. It wasn't there before. All that rain must have opened it up. He's got a sprained fetlock. I ripped up my petticoat and bandaged him with wet strips, but they'll need taking off soon or they'll do more harm than good. Put a splint on him with some dry ones and try to get him up. I'll do a fomentation when we get back to the stable."

"But Miss Lyla!" said Jeb, a stable lad who admired her and had set out to find her the minute she was reported missing. They were much the same age. "Your ankle! Is it broken? It looks awful bad!"

"I don't know. Probably. But don't worry about me. It's just that I couldn't stand up to deal with Bobby."

Needless to say, this story had gone around the village in a flash. Young Miss Lyla hadn't cried when they set her ankle (it *had* been broken). All she did was ask about her horse and if they hadn't stopped her, she would have been in the stable day and night to look after it. The boys all thought she was a real goer and any girl criticizing her was called a jealous cat.

Chapter Two

Lyla now walked past Bobby in the stables. She still rode him occasionally, but not when she needed to get anywhere quickly. He was an old horse and his fetlock had never been strong after the accident. He nickered at her as she went by and she rubbed his nose fondly.

"No, Bobby," she said. "Not today. I have to gallop. You take it easy. Firefly will tell you all about it when we get back."

Firefly was a Cleveland Bay crossed with an Andalusian and in truth, too tall for Lyla. But she loved him and he loved her. Like her, he was fearless and tireless. She'd gone with her father to the Appleby Fair when she was fifteen and had spied him there. His golden brown coat shone in the sunlight as he stood, erect and proud. She had begged and begged her father to buy him, saying she would never ask him for another thing if she could just have him. Finally, he gave in, and Firefly went home with them. Luckily, Lyla had stopped growing, since she kept her word and asked her father for nothing, not even a new gown, until two years later when her aunt came to visit.

Unbeknownst to Lyla, her mother's sister had plans to bring her out, since it was clear her father had given it no thought. She was horrified by her niece's appearance and even more horrified by Lyla's explanation. As soon as she could, she trapped her brother-in-law in his study and fired at him with both barrels.

"What can you be thinking, brother? The gown Lyla wore at dinner last night was a disgrace! It was so old it was fit for nothing but the rag basket! I heard the Vicar's wife comment on it to her husband. I declare, I could have sunk for shame!"

"She hasn't mentioned anything to me about needing a new gown. She's in riding dress most of the time, anyway."

"No, of course she hasn't. She told me she'd promised not to ask for anything if you bought her that horse."

"Good God! So she did, but I never thought she meant it!"

"Well, evidently her word means more than that of many I could mention. But she can't go around in darned and re-darned gowns more than five years out of date! I'm astonished you haven't noticed it yourself, as particular as you are about your own raiment. I came specifically to talk about what the dear girl will need for a London Season next year. It's high time for that, you realize! She's nearly nineteen! If you're not careful, she's going to end up an old maid. But now I see she needs a whole new wardrobe immediately. The Squire's May Ball is coming up, don't forget. Honestly, Digby! The neighbors must think you're in Dun Street!"

In fact, the neighbors had noticed Lyla's lack of wardrobe, but put it down to her father's selfishness rather than lack of funds.

"I suppose you're right," admitted her father. "I hadn't given it any thought."

"Well," said her aunt briskly. "I'll take her into town and have her measured for some new gowns. We can think about the London Season after that."

"For God's sake, Honoria, take it easy," said Mr. Worsley. "I'm not made of money."

"You should be, if you haven't bought your daughter — your only child — a rag to wear in over two years!"

It was thanks to her aunt that Lyla had turned up at the Squire's Ball in the new gown that became her admirably. She was not more than average height but she had a well-developed figure and her constant riding had given her an erect carriage. The rose pink silk was a lovely contrast to her dark curls and nut-brown eyes. Laurence, the future baronet, had not been the only man to notice her, but the only one she bestowed her dimpled smile upon was Harry Blankley.

The Blankleys were their nearest neighbors and Harry had been the dear friend of her youth. He was a soft-hearted boy who willingly followed her across hill and dale. He had untangled her petticoats from the brambles as unhesitatingly as his own coat; she had bound up his knee and wiped his blood on her skirts when he fell. He had hoisted her up on a wall when she was determined to get into the Squire's orchards, she had put the bait on his fishing hooks. He had once even stayed with her all night in the stables as she helped nurse a mare through a difficult foaling, though he found it distasteful and no work for a girl. She should leave it to the head groom, he said. But she ignored him.

They had been like brother and sister until he'd gone away to school, first to Eton then to Oxford. He hadn't been home much at all after that. Lyla heard from her maid Potter, who had it from the Blankleys' housekeeper, that Harry's father preferred him to spend the exeats and holidays with friends, and the word was, he did it to cut back expenses at home. Mr. Blankley Senior himself spent most of his time in London in a vain attempt to improve his finances at the gambling table.

That night at the Squire's Ball was a revelation for them both. Lyla saw her childhood friend grown into a tall, handsome man, and for him she was no longer the tomboy girl of his childhood but a desirable woman.

That summer the two old friends fell into their previous ways, albeit no longer as children. They rode out together, spent time in the stables, picked blackberries from the bushes that ran between their two properties and picnicked under the blue sky as their horses cropped at the grass beside them.

Harry was still the gentle, diffident person he had been as a boy and Lyla was sometimes irked by his lack of boldness. He said more than once he was surprised her father didn't require her to take a groom when she went out, and he didn't enjoy her neck-or-nothing gallops across the fields and, more often than not, the hedgerows. Nevertheless, by the time the autumn came, Lyla was in love.

But then Harry had been invited on a European tour with his best friend. He was reluctant to leave her, but his family, especially his father, had encouraged him to go. His mother told him no man could be really educated without such a tour. So he accepted the invitation and was away for months.

While he was away, the time came for Lyla to make her Season. She begged her father and her aunt not to make her go through with it. She knew it was nothing but a glorified Marriage Mart and though she couldn't say it, because there had been no declaration on Harry's part, she felt herself engaged to him. They thought she was just being difficult about leaving her horses.

"Not have a Season?" cried her aunt. "You don't know what you'll be missing! It's the most fun imaginable! Balls and routs and parties! You'll forget the stables in a week! And look at all the gowns we've had made for you! Don't you want to look pretty and have beaux vying for your attention?"

"No I don't, aunt! I want to stay here quietly and go on as usual. I detest balls and routs and parties and … beaux."

"Don't be ridiculous! How can you say you detest what you've no experience of? Anyway, your wardrobe is ready, your bags are packed and we're going. There's nothing more to say."

The London Season had been successful in every aspect except for the young lady's finding of a husband. When she returned home without a ring on her finger, her father had been furious. He felt he'd been cheated. He'd laid out his blunt for nothing!

In due course, Harry returned from his European tour but disappointed Lyla by not coming to see her immediately. Then, when he did come, he looked drawn and older.

"My father has allowed the family affairs to get into a dreadful state," he explained at last. "I had no idea how bad it was. We owe money to everyone. That's why he never wanted me to come home. I wish he'd taken me into his confidence before. The only solution now is for me to get a job. Make some money and try to pay off the worst of the debts before it gets any worse."

"But what sort of job?" Lyla had no experience of anything other than farming and horses and couldn't imagine what he might mean.

"I'm afraid there's nothing for me in England, but while I was in London one of my school chums said his uncle was in a fair way in some business in India. Imports and exports, or something. He needs an assistant. I'm going to write to him."

"India?" Lyla was astounded. He might as well have said the moon.

"Yes." Harry took her hands and looked in her eyes. "Lyla, you must know I love you. I couldn't say it before because... well, I've been afraid for some time the money side of things was in a bad state. But it's worse than I thought. The fact is, I can't afford to marry with the situation as it is. But if you'll wait for me, I'll put things to rights and come back for you."

"Oh yes, Harry! Yes! I'll wait for you! You know I will!"

He kissed her hands fervently but did not embrace her. "I'm not going to see your father and ask for a formal engagement, Lyla," he said. "I cannot imagine he would agree to it. It could be three or four years, or even more. Besides, it wouldn't be fair: you might meet someone else who can make you happy."

"Never!" she cried passionately. "I'll wait for you no matter how long it takes."

"And I'll always love you," he said.

Yes, thought Lyla as she strode furiously towards the stables, *that's what he'd said*: I'll always love you. *He couldn't be engaged to someone else! He couldn't!*

She saddled Firefly in a fever of impatience and left at a gallop for the Blankley estate.

Chapter Three

The voice of one of the many governesses who'd tried to turn Lyla into a lady came into her head as she neared the gates of the Blankleys' rambling house: *Never rush into a place as if the devil were on your tail, Lyla. It isn't seemly.* Why it came into her mind now, she would never be able to explain, but she was glad it did, for as she turned Firefly into the ill-kept beech-lined carriageway leading up to the front door, she reined her horse into a walk and thus came unheard upon a scene that caused her to stop altogether.

A rustic bench stood at the edge of the lawn opposite the front door. The grass was almost waist high and desperately in need of cutting, but Lyla could clearly see the couple seated there, their heads close together. She recognized Harry immediately. He was *en tête à tête* with a woman wearing what she could see even at a distance was a very modish bonnet. As Lyla watched from the shadows of the trees, Harry's mother emerged from the front door and approached the couple, holding out her hands. They stood as she came up to them and she took a hand of each, drawing them to her lips.

Lyla understood in a flash. What her father had said must be true! Harry *had* become engaged and this must be the woman! There was no other explanation. Her heart beating so loudly she was sure they must be able to hear it, Lyla forced herself to walk Firefly quietly backwards until a bend in the carriageway hid the scene from her sight. Then she turned the horse and urged him to a gallop. Her governess had said nothing about leaving a place in a rush, and even if she had, it is doubtful whether Lyla, her mind in a whirl, would have remembered it.

She arrived back home not knowing how she got there, and threw herself off her horse in front of the stables. She called automatic instructions to one of the grooms.

"Jeb! Walk Firefly for ten minutes and then give him a good rub down. Give him some fresh water after that."

Walking off in a world of her own, she didn't even hear the young man's reply. This was the same Jeb who'd found her in the ditch all those years ago. Her courage and selflessness had made him her slave forever.

"Yes, Miss. O' course. I'll give him some cut-up apple an' all. He likes that, don't you, boy?"

Jeb rubbed the sweating horse's velvety nose and took the reins. When Lyla made no response and all but ran off towards the house without a backward glance, he shook his head, puzzled. That wasn't like her at all.

A young lady always enters her home by the front door and hands her cloak and gloves to the butler. She does not dash in through the kitchens strewing her belongings behind her anyhow. This precept did not enter Lyla's mind as she ran through the back door of the house, stopping only momentarily to kick off her boots and throw off her riding gloves before dashing up the back stairs to her room. This gloomy staircase, customarily used only by the upstairs maids, suited her perfectly as it rendered invisible the tears now coming to her eyes. She barely made it to her own quarters before she was crying in earnest, great heaving sobs that she couldn't control.

She threw herself on her bed and wept as she had never wept in her life, not even at the death of her mother. She wept till she could weep no more, and lay there, spent, a headache behind her eyes. She was dying for a cup of tea, but didn't have the energy to reach for the bell to summon her maid.

She was still on her bed, listless, staring at the ceiling, when Potter found her an hour later. She had been Lyla's mother's dresser and was kept on because she was one of the few who could occasionally talk sense into a daughter who, even at that young age, had been a law unto herself. She was a plain, spare woman now in her forties and devoted to the uncontrollable girl who had turned into an uncontrollable young woman.

"Whatever are you doing, Miss Lyla, lying in the dark like that," she exclaimed. "I didn't know you were home until Gladys in the kitchen said she'd seen you run through earlier like you were being chased by the devil himself."

Then coming closer and lighting the candles, she saw her face, almost as white as the pillows on which she lay. "But you're still in your riding dress! Are you ailing, Miss Lyla? You look dreadful! What's the matter?"

"Nothing, Potter, really. Don't fuss. I had a... a long ride and felt weary. I've just got a bit of a headache, that's all. A cup of tea will put me right, if you would bring one. And please tell cook I won't be down for dinner. The Squire's coming tonight, I believe. He and Papa will enjoy it more if I'm not there to force them to mind their manners and their stories."

While her maid was gone, Lyla splashed her face in the cold water on the washstand and brushed her hair into a neat knot on top of her head. Tendrils framed her face, as they usually did, but she took so little notice of her own face, she did not see how well they became her, even with her pallor. She took off her riding skirt and jacket and slipped on a shapeless dimity dress she never wore outside the confines of her own room. Potter returned with a pot of tea and a plate of small biscuits, then took off the riding dress for a brushing, leaving her young mistress alone.

By the time dinner was served to her on a tray, Lyla had formed a plan. Her father wouldn't like it, but she thought she could persuade him. It did not mean she was able to pass a restful night, however. It seemed to her she heard the hall clock strike every hour.

The following morning she went down to breakfast when she was sure her father would have finished his meal, determined to speak to him before he went out again. Like most countrymen, he always breakfasted after the morning rounds. He was sitting at the table, the remains of an ample meal spread before him, frowning at the pages in a ledger.

"Good morning, father," she began.

Before she could go any further, he looked up and said, "Well, it's exactly as I told you. Young Blankley is engaged to the Warner girl. Squire ate his mutton here last night and he told me. Everyone's talking about it. I hope you didn't ride over there and make a fool of yourself."

"No, Papa, I didn't. I... I found out about it and came home."

"Good. Now just you give serious consideration to Foxworthy's proposal. You could do a lot worse. He's well set-up, got a tidy little place over there by Ickenham and said everything proper when he came to see me. Settlements and so on."

"I told you yesterday, Papa. I shall never marry Mr. Foxworthy. I'm sure he's very eligible and will make someone a wonderful husband, but not me. I don't love him."

"Love? Mush! Love will come. You marry him and have yourself a couple of babies and you'll see."

"No, Papa. I will not see. Anyway, I've an idea I want to talk to you about. I've been thinking…"

But she was unable to say what she was thinking, this time because the butler came with his silent tread into the room and announced, "If I may interrupt you, sir, Mr. Blankley is begging a word with Miss Lyla. I've put him in the small parlor."

At the sound of the name, Lyla started up and said urgently, "No, Fulton! I cannot see him! Please tell Mr. Blankley I'm indisposed.. I… I am not feeling well. I… I…" and she ran from the room.

Her father looked at the old retainer and shrugged. "You heard what she said, Fulton. Tell the young cub Miss Lyla won't see him." He shook his head and sighed. "Women!" and he turned back to his ledger.

Chapter Four

Lyla fled back to her room and sat on her bed, pushing her knuckles into her mouth in an effort to hold back her tears. She longed to see Harry, to ask him why he had broken his promise, but she knew she would break down if she did. And she was determined not to cry any more. No man who had gone back on his word was worth it. Then she straightened her back and clenched her teeth. It was over.

When she was sure Harry had left — in fact, she knew he had because she hadn't been able to stop herself peeping through the heavy curtains to watch him leave, riding the big old roan she knew so well — Lyla went to the stables and saddled up Firefly. Like the day before, she took off at a gallop, but in the opposite direction, wanting to get as far away from the Blankley estate as possible. She gave the horse its head, not caring how far she went, or where.

In the early afternoon it was almost a relief to find herself hungry. She had eaten no breakfast and had missed lunch, but it surprised her she could feel anything other than heartache.

Arriving back home, she took her usual passage through the kitchen. She took a hunk of cheese, a large slice of bread and a pear from the larder and sat down at the kitchen table to eat it. No one was surprised. It wasn't the first time Miss Lyla had ridden out too far to return for lunch and had satisfied her hunger with whatever she could find.

When she had finished her meal, she went to find her maid in the small parlor that had been her domain since Lyla's mother's time.

"Please have the girls bring hot water up for a bath, Potter," she said. "I'm dreadfully dirty and I'm afraid my riding dress is even worse."

"Of course. And don't you worry about your dress, Miss Lyla. I'll see to it, though I'm thinking it's high time you had a new one."

"Perhaps you're right. It is dreadfully shabby." Lyla began to walk away, but then turned back and said, "Potter, if I were to leave here and go far away, would you come with me? "

"Of course, Miss Lyla." The answer came without hesitation. "What else would I do? There'd be nothing here for me without you."

"Dear Potter!" Lyla hugged her maid impulsively. "But I don't want you to say that because you think you should. I have no right to take you away. This is your home, after all."

"It wouldn't be my home if you weren't here, Miss Lyla. Where you go, I go."

Lyla hugged her again and went up the back stairs to her room.

In London some of the newer homes had rooms with a bathtub permanently installed, though the maids still had to carry up ewers of hot and cold water to fill it. Here, though, a footman had to first carry up a zinc tub, and then it took several trips for the maids to bring up the water.

While all this activity was going on, Lyla sat on the edge of her bed trying to forget the sight of Harry's mother bringing the couple's fingers to her lips. She was no doubt delighted her son had found an heiress who could save the family from ruin. Much better than a countrywoman whose only claim to fame was that she could pick a horse as well as any man and ride one better than most.

But Harry! What could have made him change his mind about going to India? Was it possible he had fallen in love and forgotten her so easily? She couldn't believe it! Now she half wished she had seen him that morning. She could have had it out with him and at least her mind would be rid of these nagging conjectures.

Potter was surprised when Lyla said she would put on her best evening gown. Thanks to her London season, she now had an extensive wardrobe. It included several pretty day and evening dresses and no fewer than three ball gowns. Since her return from the capital she was again spending her days in riding dress and rarely wore anything but the least costly evening gown for dinner. But tonight she put on her best. It was royal blue silk with a deep flounce of ivory lace around the sleeves and inset under the bosom. Because of the lace, it had cost almost as much as the ballgown and her father had frowned at the bill. But he admitted it became her very well and was pleased to have her wear it on the few occasions they were invited out.

In her lovely gown and with her curls fastened elegantly on top of her head, Lyla swept into the drawing room looking a good deal more confident than she felt.

Her father instinctively rose to his feet.

"'Pon my word, Lyla, you look mighty fine tonight for your old Papa!"

"I thought I was a shame to only put on my finery when we see other people. You are more important than anyone else, after all!" She kissed his cheek.

"I'm relieved you're not weeping over young Blankley."

"I, weeping? You know me better than that, Papa."

"So you'll have Foxworthy, after all?"

"No, Papa. I told you I wouldn't and I won't. But I have another plan."

She took a deep breath.

"I want you to let me go to Ireland. You were telling me just the other day that Seamus must be getting too old. The last horses he sent us were below par, and the lot before that not much better. Let me go and do the buying! You know I can!"

"Don't be ridiculous! You can't go to Newbridge! They'd laugh at you trying to buy a dog, let alone a horse!"

"That's what you said when I went to Barnet alone last year because you were laid up with a putrid sore throat. I got a good haul, including Galahad, and you've got to admit, he did us proud."

"A fluke. Or the seller was taken by your dimples."

"No it wasn't, but even if it was, why shouldn't the Irish sellers be taken by my dimples too? Look, Papa, I'm telling you here and now I'm never going to marry. So unless you want me at home for the rest of my life you have to give me something to do elsewhere. Newbridge is the obvious choice. Seamus clearly needs help. I need something to do. I know as much about horses as he does." She almost added, "and more than you do," but decided that wouldn't win her case. "Why don't you let me go for, say eighteen months? We'll see if it works out. If it doesn't, I'll come back."

Digby Worsley stopped walking around the room. He sighed heavily.

"I wish your poor mother was here to talk to you. It seems such a waste. You're nice-looking and you've got the ... the... well," and he had the grace to look abashed, "you're not too thin to bear me a healthy grandson. But I can't deny Seamus isn't sending us what we need and it's true you're as good as any man when it comes to choosing a horse."

He sighed again.

"Very well. I'll give you a year. But I want you back then, and you'll marry a man I choose. I won't be left without a grandson. I'll write to Seamus and tell him I'm sending you to help out temporarily. He can use you as a scout. Let you do the footwork and when you find anything worthwhile, you send for him to take a look. God knows what he'll say, but at least you can't do any harm."

Lyla hardly listened to the first part of his answer. She threw her arms around her father's neck and kissed him on his cheek. "Thank you, Papa! I won't let you down."

He smelled of bay and mint, a concoction he always used. It was he, not she, who favored beauty aids.

Chapter Five

Her father always enjoyed a hand or two of cards after dinner, and though she usually tried to avoid it, that night she indulged him. He tended to be erratic in his play, sometimes making brilliant moves, but they were almost always followed by a series of blunders. It made him a trying opponent and a disastrous partner. That night, however his luck was in, or his mood more mellow, for he played well and ending up winning.

"By God," he said. "I wish I'd been playing with the Squire tonight. He won a pony off me yesterday. I'd have had it back!"

Lyla was glad he was in a good mood. She was dreading he might change his mind about her gong to Ireland, so she replied, "You played brilliantly Papa. I'm sorry you didn't have a better opponent."

"Oh well, women rarely have a head for cards, m'dear." He kissed her cheek as they left the drawing room to go up to bed.

Under normal circumstances, Lyla would have retorted that women were just as clever as men, cleverer, really, if one considered they hardly ever had the educational opportunities men had. But tonight she smiled acquiescence.

They were in the hall when the butler approached her with an envelope in his hand.

"This arrived for you earlier, Miss Lyla, but I was told you were, …er, engaged, so I didn't have it sent up. It's been on the hall table all evening. I'm sorry. I should have brought it to you before."

Lyla had recognized the handwriting immediately. It was from Harry. She forced herself to accept it nonchalantly and tucked it in her sleeve.

"Ah, yes, it's from the Vicar's wife. She's been promising me a recipe for pickled mushrooms this age. She must finally have remembered. Thank you, Fulton."

Since Lyla took no notice at all of what went on in the kitchen and would rather receive a recipe for a horse liniment than for pickled mushrooms, it's possible that neither man believed her. But they made no comment. Nonetheless, it took all her willpower to calmly kiss her father goodnight, walk slowly up the stairs, and go slowly to her room.

But at last she was alone. She stared at the envelope. What could Harry possibly have written? He could say nothing that would explain his perfidy. She should just put it on the fire and forget he ever existed. Twice she tried to do so, and twice she pulled her hand back from the flames. Finally, realizing she could not live without knowing what was in the letter, she opened the envelope.

My dearest Lyla,

I know you must have heard about my engagement to Miss Warner and that's why you refused to see me this morning. They said you were indisposed and could not come, but I have never known you indisposed and I could guess the truth. I know you so well, my dear.

I told you that my father had put my family into peril by his mismanagement. We owe a great deal of money. I could have dealt with that. I had already been in touch with our creditors and used the little money left to me by my uncle to pay the most pressing debts. For the rest, they had agreed to payment over time. I was to go to

India and send quarterly remittances. We were to lease our lands, sell our livestock and my family was to live in a quiet way until I could return.

What I did not know was that my father had been gambling. He said it was the only way he could see of getting us out of our difficulties. But instead of that, he made the situation worse, much worse. He staked our fields, our pastures and finally the house itself, and lost everything! And gambling debts, I'm sure you know, must be paid at once. He came home last week and confessed it all. My mother and sisters were to pack up and move — heaven knows where — because the new owners were coming to claim the property almost immediately.

I became acquainted with Daphne Warner in London last year. We met frequently at parties and routs, and, well, to be frank, I knew she would have been pleased to have me pay her my addresses. I did not, for the reasons you're well aware of. She is a considerable heiress herself, though her family's fortune was made in trade. I believe her grandfather was a wine merchant. The word is, he was lucky with his investments on the 'Change. As you know, ours is a very old family and though we are impecunious, we have a family tree going back to the Normans. In any case, I came home and saw you again, my dearest friend who soon became my dearest love. I no longer thought of Daphne.

When I heard the dreadful news about losing our home, I admit, I panicked. My poor dear mother and sisters! I should have come to see you to explain, but I was like a madman. I rode immediately to London and sought an interview with Daphne's father. Except in one *issue, I was straight with him. I told him the trouble my family was in. But to my eternal shame I told him I loved his daughter and it was only the knowledge of my family's situation that had stopped me addressing him before. You know that was not true, and I shall carry the dishonor of that lie to the grave. I love you, Lyla. I always have, and I always will.*

Daphne, God bless her, received me with joy and agreed at once to become my wife. Her father willingly redeemed my father's vowels and I brought her back with me as my fiancée to meet Mama and my sisters. She is an only child and is delighted with the idea of having sisters.

You would like her, Lyla. She is kind and loving. I know she will make me a good wife. I only hope I can make her a good husband. It will be hard, knowing that I have let you down, but I am persuaded your generosity will make you understand that I have to act in my family's interest, not my own.

Forgive me, Lyla.

Your devoted friend,
Harry.

Lyla put the letter in her lap and stared ahead, unseeing. Harry said she would understand. But did she? Would she have done the same in his place? Probably. Possibly. Perhaps. Or would she have allowed the folly of a parent to take its course, to lose the family estate, to make shift as best she could, if it meant the person she loved was by her side? Yes, she thought she would. If only she had Harry, she would consider it all well lost. But it wasn't up to her. She had nothing to say in the matter. They had never been formally engaged. He had said she might not want to wait for him, but it turned out, it was he who did not wait for her.

Chapter Six

Harry and Daphne were married in London a month later. Lyla tried to avoid all reports of the wedding, and when Harry's mother wrote her a cordial note asking her to tea, she replied that she was in the midst of packing for a long journey and was unfortunately unable to come. But on Sunday after church she was unable to avoid the vicar's wife.

"Oh, my dear!" said she, "What a shame you missed Mrs. Blankley's tea, especially as you could not be at the wedding due to that rash keeping you indoors for a week. And you and Harry such good friends! By all accounts the lace on the bride's gown cost a king's ransom, the wedding breakfast was the finest money could buy and Harry was the handsomest man in the place, walking down the aisle with his new wife on his arm. I can well believe it, can not you?"

"Yes, indeed, Ma'am." Lyla struggled to keep her composure. "I'm sure he was. But I must be off. We anticipate a mare foaling this afternoon, and I'm a little worried about it."

"How many times I've told your father it's not fitting a girl like you assisting in such matters. I'm sure your poor mama would not have liked it."

"On the contrary, Ma'am," Lyla replied, more tartly that she had ever spoken to the older woman before, "If more girls saw the realities of birth it would prepare them for later. At least they would know what to expect."

And she walked swiftly away, leaving the woman to shake her head and comment, as so many before and so many after, that she didn't know what the younger generation was coming to.

It was inconceivable, of course, that Lyla should travel alone to Ireland. When she set off at the end of the summer, it was with her maid Potter and the groom Jeb, whom her father had agreed to let go. When he found out she was leaving, he begged to be allowed to go with her.

"For y'know, Miss, you might need a man's protection."

Looking at his frame, which was still boyishly skinny, she smiled to herself but answered him with all seriousness.

"That's true, Jeb, but to tell you the truth I think I'll need you more for just plain hard work. But are you sure you want to leave home? We may well be gone for a long time." *Forever* was what she said to herself, but didn't utter.

"That's all right w' me. I want to see somethin' of the world. Never bin anywhere and now's me chance."

Jeb rode up next to the driver of the Mail coach that took them from London to Liverpool, and such was his excitement that in spite of his earlier protestations, the welfare of the two women was entirely forgotten. When an inebriated solicitor's clerk boarded the coach at Birmingham and attempted to kiss her, it was Lyla herself who delivered a well-aimed kick at his shin. When they made the brief stops for refreshment allowed by the Mail, it was Potter who scrambled for a cup of tea for herself and her mistress, and when they arrived at the overnight inns where rooms had been bespoken, it was some time before anyone could find Jeb and remind him to see to their trunks. He had wandered off to look at the new railway tracks and would have stayed there all night waiting for a train to pass.

On the boat from Liverpool to Dublin, he was fearfully sick from the moment the vessel left shore until it touched it again on the other side and it was they who had to minister to him. He was immensely relieved at the sight of a bright red lighthouse at the entrance to Dublin Harbor as they arrived, but could barely listen to the explanations of an aged crew member before retching over the side — again. The sailor looked too old to lift a teacup but hopped nimbly about the deck talking in his musically accented English to anyone who would listen.

"Aye, yon's ole Poolbeg," he explained. "Her went up fifty year ago when Oi were a lad, so she did. Tis t'end o' the harbor wall y'see. They've been after building of it most of me life. Afore that ye couldn't get next or nigh the city in a big boat like t'is. T' harbor got filled up, y'see."

The last bit puzzled her until another passenger explained he was talking about the sand that apparently flowed incessantly into Dublin harbor before the construction of the walls, making it impassable for deep-keeled vessels.

In fact, the appearance of the whole port amazed her. They were sailing towards a green-domed white Palladian building of classical proportions. Lyla had never been to Rome, but from the illustrations she remembered in her school books, she thought it wouldn't look out of place there. Behind it, other construction was going on and as they drew nearer, she could see crowds of men on the docks, loading and unloading cattle, coal, and boxes by the hundreds. It was a hive of activity. The whole place was far from the backwater she had imagined.

The white palace turned out to be the Customs House, where, in due course, they presented themselves. They had nothing to declare except Firefly, who had come on the long journey with them. It was foolish, she knew, to bring a horse to Ireland, where her whole business was to be buying them, but she couldn't bear to leave him behind.

The journey had only been three days in a well-sprung coach and with a smooth crossing, but they were all tired and longing to spend twenty-four hours in a place that wasn't rocking under their feet. Lyla was exhausted. She had been unable to get a moment's rest, but not because of the rocking. The minute she shut her eyes, the vision of Harry and Daphne on the bench assaulted her. A vice would grip her heart and she could scarcely breathe. Then the effort of trying to appear carefree made it worse. She just wanted to go to a quiet, dark place, curl up and never move again.

But they still had to make the twenty-five mile journey to Newbridge. To convey them there, her father's agent Seamus O'Donoghue sent a coach that back at home would have been considered unfit for a lady to travel in. Potter raised her eyebrows when she saw it, but, resigned to yet more jolting and too tired to care, Lyla just climbed wearily in. Jeb was so pleased to be back on dry land he got up beside the driver without complaint and was soon chattering excitedly and exclaiming at everything he saw. He was able to report to them, when they stopped at an inn to rest the horses and have a bite to eat, that the man's name was Padraig.

"Seems a good enough bloke, Miss, once you can get yer 'ead around what 'e's saying. Good with the 'orses."

The lumbering old coach had been sent because it was the largest vehicle Mr. O'Donoghue had. He'd said if he knew females, they'd have the divil's own mountain of luggage. And it was true, they did. They had eight trunks and numerous bandboxes filled with things Potter had considered essential for a lady's comfort. All Lyla had wanted was to leave as soon as possible and she would have taken practically nothing. But Potter had set her lip firmly and told her she would pack what was required and that was all there was to it.

The coach journey was very uncomfortable. The windows were jammed open, leaving them exposed to the damp and wind that they soon learned was more or less a permanent feature of the weather there. Even though the road out of the city was a toll road and well maintained, such springs as the coach had were beyond their useful life, so weak as to make any bump in the road lift them clean off the seats. This was made all the more uncomfortable because the seat padding was in parts worn down to the bare wood. More than once, Lyla thought she'd be better riding Firefly who was attached to the rear of the coach and trotting amiably behind. But she had no idea in which trunk her riding dress was packed, and Potter wouldn't tell her.

"You'll not ride behind the carriage, Miss Lyla! Whoever heard of a lady doing such a thing! I can't imagine what your poor dear mother would say."

Lyla knew that whenever Potter invoked her mother, that was the end of the discussion.

The further they got from Dublin, the poorer both the road and the surroundings became, though Lyla took little notice. Potter, however, was shocked at the poverty of the dwellings they passed.

"Look at the way the people are living," she said as they passed a low cottage into which a farmer appeared to be driving a small herd of cows. "They even live with their animals!"

Dublin had been a flourishing city, with a number of white buildings in the same style as the Customs House. But now the city was behind them, things were very different. The dwellings were very simple thatched constructions made of wattle and daub. They had only one window, or sometimes none, and often sloped at the back. It was into one of these they saw a pig and two cows being driven.

"I suppose it keeps everyone warmer," said Lyla. "I don't blame them, in this climate. It's not exactly cold, but it's so damp!" She pulled her cloak closer around her. "And I suppose the slope would make the animal waste flow away. That's a good idea."

"I hope we're not going to live with the horses," said Potter.

Lyla smiled wearily. "No, of course not!" Papa said Seamus has hired a house for us. Perhaps it's like one of those white mansions in Dublin."

Chapter Seven

The light was almost gone from the sky when they crossed a wide dark river and turned onto a road which took them in front of a high wall pierced by a tall gate. The stone wall ran in both directions and uniformed sentries were posted on either side of the gate. Behind it they could see the outline of a church and other tall buildings topped by multiple chimney pots.

"It must be a garrison," said Lyla. "And to judge from the establishments opposite, the soldiers are well provided with entertainment."

As she spoke, a raucous group erupted from a doorway and a tangle of men fell into the road, flailing, fighting and swearing.

Potter shuddered. "I hope to goodness we won't be living anywhere near this!"

Her hope seemed to be well founded, for they continued down the road until the wall was no longer on their left. But soon after, the coach drew to a halt. They were in front of a long, plain, single story white edifice set a little back from the road. Across the road from it were some shuttered shops, but there was nothing in the least resembling a Palladian mansion or, indeed, a recognizable house of any kind. Lyla couldn't understand why they'd stopped.

"Is this Newbridge?" she asked.

The answer was both clear and mystifying.

"We come over t' new bridge, so we did, Missus." This was accompanied by a wave of the arm back the way they had come.

"Yes, I understand there's a new bridge. But where is Newbridge?"

The driver repeated the same explanation, and Lyla finally understood that there wasn't actually a place called Newbridge. They were simply going to live near the new bridge and the unlikely looking building in front of them was evidently to be their home.

The door was opened to them by a woman who in the light of the oil lamp she held, had a cheerful, round-cheeked countenance. She smiled and bobbed a curtsey.

"Sure and you'll be Miss Lyla," she said in a lilting Irish accent. "And a welcome to you! I'm Brigid. Do you come on in out of t' cold."

She led them into a long dark room which appeared to be lit only by her oil lamp and a faintly glowing hearth. A sweet, earthy smell was the first thing that hit Lyla's nose and under it, a welcome scent of something cooking. Brigid placed the lamp on a table. In the pool of yellow light they could see four mismatched wooden chairs but beyond that, except for the soft glow in the hearth, all was shadow. Lyla walked towards the fire. The odd sweet odor became stronger and she realized it came from the fire itself. The smell of cooking emanated from a black pot hanging over it. Her stomach rumbled and she was surprised to find she was hungry. Until then the stress and anxiety of the trip had destroyed her appetite.

Jeb came in carrying the first of their trunks. He looked around. "Padraig said this place was fer the men what built the garrison. Not the soldiers. The ones what had to come and stop 'ere while they was building. That's why it's not inside the walls."

"So it was a dormitory for working men?" Lyla was astonished.

"Yuss. Padraig said the King's Dragoons come 'ere bout eighteen months ago. The locals weren't too keen on 'em. Still ain't, by all 'counts. The brickies and chippies needed the work but din't want to live in the barracks, so they built this place."

He disappeared and came back a few minutes later with another trunk. He put it down and turned to Lyla.

"There's some snug stables in the back. Padraig's seein' to Firefly. Like I said, 'e's good with 'orses."

Brigid had by now lit a candle on the table and bustled off into the black depths beyond, where she set down the lantern. The light cast fantastic shadows through the doorway of what must have been the scullery. She reappeared with a tray carrying a huge brown pot and a collection of pewter mugs. She set these on the table and left again, coming back with a bowl of sugar, a loaf of bread and a dish of pale yellow butter.

Padraig reappeared at the door and gave Lyla a vague salute.

"Sure an' I'll be off for me dinner at the minute. Mr. O'Donoghue said to tell you he'd be by in t' mornin'."

"Thank you, Padraig," said Lyla with a smile. You've been such a help." She picked up the reticule she'd put on the table and found a sixpence, which she gave to him. "I'm afraid I don't have any Irish pence."

"T'all spends, Missus," he replied. "Evenin' Brigid!" he called into the scullery and with another salute was gone.

Brigid reappeared as the door closed. "He'll be off up the road fer a jar, so he will," she commented. "An there's his wife's got a nice rabbit pie all ready for his dinner. Men!" she shook her head.

Then coming to the table set with the tea and bread, she said, "Will you and the other lady be after taking a mug o' tay, Miss? You must be parched as well as frozen! The dinner can simmer till all your traps be brought in."

"Thank you, Brigid. This lady is Miss Potter. She's my... companion. We'll both take tea, if you please, and I daresay Jeb wouldn't say no either."

"A lad like him's more likely to take a mug o' homebrew, I'm tinkin'. There's a barrel in the back Mr. O'Donoghue dropped off earlier."

Sure enough, when Jeb came in with bandboxes in both hands, he declared a pint of homebrew would set him up proper, and he followed Brigid into the shadowy depths, emerging a few moments later with a foaming mug.

"Let's all sit down," said Lyla, "before this tea gets cold." She pulled out a chair and suited the action to the word. Potter sat willingly, but Jeb hopped from one foot to the other while Brigid poured the tea and cut some slices of bread.

"It don't feel right I should sit along a' you in all me dirt, Miss Lyla," he said. "I'll just drink up and get on w' the boxes an' all."

"Very well, but later when we have our dinner we shall all sit together," said Lyla. "Brigid will show you where you can wash your hands and you shall eat with us here. Many's the time I've eaten in the kitchen at home, and I don't see why you shouldn't eat in the dining room now, if this is what this is. Now, take a piece of bread and butter with you. You must be hungry."

"I am that," said Jeb, willingly taking the doorstep of bread Brigid cut for him and liberally slathered with butter.

The ladies gratefully drank a mug of tea and ate a (much thinner) slice of bread and butter. Their eyes were accustomed to the gloom by now and in the back of the room they could make out the dark shapes of two beds. This was obviously where they were to sleep. Lyla couldn't help smiling. Their dwelling was evidently just this one room with a scullery attached. And she had imagined living in a Palladian mansion!

Chapter Eight

Though her last thoughts as she closed her eyes were, as always, of Harry, for the first night since the awful day she'd seen him with his betrothed, Lyla slept quite well. But when she woke into the grey light of morning, her mind again flew to him. Was he happy? Was his wife kind to him? And inevitably, did he miss her? The leaden weight on her heart had become so familiar it felt part of her.

The beds were rustic affairs made up of a feather mattress over a lattice of ropes. They had brought their own linen in one of the trunks Jeb unloaded, and while the stew simmered she and Potter had made up the beds. They unpacked their nightgowns but left everything else where it was. There were rows of pegs along the walls but it was too dark to see properly, and besides, they were both too worn out to unpack completely.

Jeb did sit down with them at dinner the night before, though it clearly made him uncomfortable. Not so uncomfortable that he didn't make a hearty meal of the stew. It proved to be mostly potatoes and carrots with the occasional piece of mutton, but the gravy was thick and delicious. They were all hungry and glad of it.

When questioned about where Jeb would sleep, Brigid shrugged and said, "Sure an' he'll do fine in the stalls out back."

Jeb fully agreed.

"Will you be comfortable?" worried Lyla.

"Don't worry, Miss. I'll bundle meself in the straw, and Firefly 'n me, we'll be as snug as yer like. There's a fireplace at one end, but I won't bother with it t'night. Need to take a gander at the chimbley first. But I'll be all right. Don't you fret."

"Remember, we saw those people living with their animals," Potter reminded her.

In spite of this, Lyla insisted he take a couple of the quilts they'd brought. Now, next to thinking about Harry, she wondered how Jeb would pass the night. She was, after all, responsible for both him and Potter.

She woke to the grey light of morning and was surprised the room was still quite warm. Brigid told her the night before that the people in those parts burned peat, or turf, rather than wood. That explained the sweet, earthy smell. The peat, which they dug in slabs from the marshy land all around, was easier to obtain, cheaper and burned longer. Before leaving, Brigid had built up what she called *a block* with peat and ashes, saying, "It'll be burning slow all night, so t'will. You'll see."

Lyla got up, put on her boots, pulled a heavy shawl around her shoulders and went to look at the fire. As she crossed the room, she saw that the morning light was coming in through a row of narrow barred windows up high in the wall opposite the hearth. They'd been hidden in the shadows the night before. The whitewashed wall under them had a row of pegs like the ones they had noticed next to their beds. She surmised that there would have been a row of cots all along the wall for the men, each with its own peg. Presumably the bars on the windows were for security. The dwelling was probably excellent for its original purpose, but it was far from a suitable home for a lady.

By now the fire looked like nothing but a large pile of ash, but there was still considerable warmth coming from it. There was a stack of peat next to the hearth but she didn't know whether to put more on the fire, as she would with logs, or leave it alone. While she hesitated, she heard a door opening in the scullery and was pleased when Brigid stuck her head into the room.

"Och, tis up y'are already, Miss. Sure an' I was hopin' t' have breakfast ready for you."

She came to the hearth, put down the large basket she was carrying and poked heartily at the pile of ash, moving most of it away from the center of the fire. Then she stood fresh turf on its ends, making a tent shape, and pushed some of the ashes back next to it. Small flames began to lick at the edges of the peat. She pushed the rest of the ashes into the center.

"We don't want it to flame up," she said. "Just smolder nice an' slow. An' the kettle in the scullery won't take long t'boil. 'Tis already warm. I made you some *blaa* for breakfast. I joost need to bake 'em up."

She bent down to her basket and took out a napkin that she unwrapped to reveal a number of small round rolls. Off to the side of the hearth was a black dish with a domed lid. Brigid took the dome off, placed the rolls on the bottom and replaced the cover. Then she pushed the whole contraption into the ashes.

Lyla was fascinated by the way things were cooked, as well as the speed and efficiency with which Brigid accomplished it. Back at home they'd had a Rumford stove for years, and though the old cook complained about it all the time, even she said it was a huge improvement on cooking over the hearth. Like most old folks, she liked to compare what things were like when she was a young woman, and often told the kitchen maids how much harder it had been in her day.

"If you saw what we 'ad to do when I were a girl," she used to say, "it'd make yer 'air curl. Carryin' about them big 'eavy pots, putting 'em on an' orf the fire all day long. You young'uns don't know yer born!"

But Brigid accomplished it all without any fuss or bother, then straightened her back and walked back to the scullery, wiping her hands on her apron.

Lyla followed her. She'd only had the vaguest impression of it the night before but now daylight was coming in through a row of barred windows like those in the main room, she could see that, like the rest of the dwelling, it was simply furnished. A kettle hung over a fireplace that was smaller than the one in the main room, and under the high windows stood a big stone sink with a sloping draining table next to it. A collection of buckets and ewers were in a row underneath. In the corner, a dresser held pewter bowls and mugs and the huge teapot. A square pine table with a couple of wooden stools stood in the center of the room. A pile of potatoes and a cabbage lay on top, scattered with mouse droppings. Brigid saw her looking at them.

"Aye. T' mice've found us already. I'll be after gettin' you a cat. Me mam's got a good mouser that just had a litter. I'll bring them over with the mother cat. She'll show the littl'uns how to do it, and when they're big enough, we'll keep a couple."

There was a knock at the scullery door and Jeb poked his head around. Lyla drew her shawl more tightly around herself to cover her nightgown.

"Oh, beg pardon, Miss!" Jeb averted his eyes. "I were just seein' if Brigid wants I should draw more water from the well. Firefly's fed and watered. 'E were tuckered out same as us after the trip. I'm leavin' 'im to rest."

"Thank you Jeb. Yes, please bring in more water. I'm sure we're going to need it. Then come in and have some breakfast. Brigid's baking some delicious-looking rolls." Remembering his discomfort the evening before, she added, "You can eat here in the kitchen."

When he was gone, Lyla turned to Brigid. "Miss Potter and I will want to wash up next door. I'm going to have to put up a curtain or something for privacy."

"Do you go on back, Miss. Shut the scullery door. I'll be after bringing you a bucket o' water. Don't you worry. No one will come next or nigh you till you give the word."

Lyla went back to find Potter up, dressed and making the beds. She frowned when she saw Lyla in her nightgown.

"It isn't seemly for you to wander about like that, Miss Lyla. Anyone could see you!"

"Not unless they're a giraffe. Look how high the windows are!"

Lyla had seen illustrations of these animals in books as a child and had giggled at the time thinking how useful they would be for rescuing people from towers. Rapunzel, for example. She'd always thought how much it must have hurt, having the prince tug at her hair while climbing up it.

Brigid came in with a pail of water. "I put a nice bit 'a hot in to take the chill off, Miss. The blaa's jist about baked and t' kettle's boilin'. Soon as you're ready, I'll make tea, so I will."

"Give me two shakes and I'll be done. Though I do feel conspicuous washing in what amounts to the parlor!"

"Hmpf! Not like any parlor I ever saw," said Potter.

Chapter Nine

The tea and blaa rolls were delicious: hot and sweet on the one hand and warm and buttered on the other. They could hear Jeb chattering to Brigid in the kitchen. He presented himself a little later praising the quality of the rolls he had polished off and saying he was going to try his hand at shooting a couple of rabbits for their dinner. It seemed the inhabitants of the building, which belonged to the King, had the right to hunt on what was the King's land. He returned a couple of hours later with two fine big animals which Brigid rapidly dealt with, then put them with some onions and potatoes into the large black pot over the smoldering fire.

"'Tis a pity the fireplace in the scullery is so small, no room for much more than a kettle o'water," remarked Bridget. "I'm tinkin' the men did no cookin' in there. Probly joost went to the pub!"

"I'm glad the bigger fireplace is in here," said Lyla. "It's warmer and we can smell our delicious dinner cooking!"

The two ladies spent the rest of the morning unpacking such of their belongings as they could find a place to put away. The beds were soon piled high. Potter looked around helplessly.

"Where I'm to put the bedlinens and tablecloths, not to mention the napkins, I don't know!" she said. "And your mother's dinner service, what am I to do with it?"

"You didn't bring that?" Lyla could hardly believe her ears.

"Certainly I did. The service belongs to you and it should go where you go. Just like your mother's linens with the embroidered S (her mother's maiden name had been Swaythling). Who's going to shake the moth out of it all regular like I do? I couldn't trust any of the girls at home to do it."

She didn't add her fear that Lyla's father, bereft of company, might find himself a wife. Men like him, fearing the approach of old age, often did. And a wife, well, Potter wouldn't put it past any female not to appropriate Miss Lyla's belongings.

"We can put the gowns on the pegs along the walls," suggested Lyla. "It will look like a drapery shop, but at least they'll be off the beds. I'm afraid you'll have to leave the linens and the china service in the trunks for the time being. And our undergarments. I suppose we can't display those!" She laughed at the thought. "It would make the place look like a different sort of establishment altogether!"

Potter wrinkled her brow, then, understanding what she had meant, said "Miss *Lyla*!" in a scandalized tone. She slowly repacked the linens in the trunks they had come out of.

"Oh, Miss Lyla," she said suddenly, sinking onto her bed, which apart from the wooden chairs at the table, was the only thing to sit on, "I never thought it would come to this. How are we to live in such a place? There's no refinement, no comfort, not even any furniture! What would your dear mother say, if she saw it?"

Lyla put her arms around her. "Well, you knew her better than I, Potter dear, but I like to think she would say the women in our family were up to any challenge. And we are! I promise it will all work out."

A sharp knock on the door made them both jump. Lyla ran over and opened it to a gentleman whose bulk filled the doorway. Bushy grey hair sprang out from beneath his top hat and merged with an equally bushy grey beard, so his whole face appeared to be set in a thicket of grey. The face itself was riddled with blue-red veins and the almost purple nose was bulbous. But his nut-brown eyes twinkled at her in such a merry fashion that she could not help but smile in response.

"Seamus O'Donoghue," he announced. "I din't come earlier for fear o' disturbing you ladies at your toy-let."

Lyla laughed. "I'm Lyla Worsley." She held out her hand. "And let me tell you any toilette would have been difficult in a place where there's nowhere for a lady to even lay her hairbrush!"

"Whisht! Don't say it! Tis lovely y'are, hairbroosh or no."

Without waiting to be invited in, Mr. O'Donoghue waddled into the room and looked around.

"Why! Tis a home already!" he declared. "An' will y' look at all t' pretty gowns! Sure an' it makes a man's heart beat fast jist t' see 'em a-hanging by the wall!"

"That's as may be, Mr. O'Donoghue," said Lyla. "But it has quite a different effect upon a lady. She does not like to see her wardrobe displayed for visitors. If this is the best place you can find for us, I'm afraid we are going to need a good deal more furniture to live here with any degree of comfort. But won't you sit and have a cup of tea? I'm sure Brigid can revive the leaves in the pot."

"Tay, is it? Not a bit of it! Let me tell you, Miss Lyla, when a gentleman comes a-callin' he'll be after a drop 'o something a sight better than tay!"

"Well, we have nothing better and we don't expect any gentlemen to come calling, other than yourself, of course."

"Whisht!" responded their visitor, "As soon as his Majesty's men next door find out you're here, we'll have to put an armed sentry by the door to hold 'em back!"

"I certainly hope that isn't true!" cried Lyla, alarmed. "I don't have time to deal with unwanted callers and I will not have Miss Potter bothered by them. Can't you put out the word an old lady with warts has come to live here and she'll put a spell on anyone who crosses her threshold?"

"Now, Miss Lyla, I'm what you might call *in lokee parentee* and it's my dewty to tell you, you can't be funning about sich things around here. Folks don't like to hear about the spells. Afore you know where y'are, they'll be burning the place down, with you in it! Anywise, one look at ye and they'll see you're a lovely alanna, so y'are."

"Oh dear! Was this truly all you could find for us, Mr. O'Donoghue? Apparently it was built as a workmen's dormitory!"

"Now, let's not be havin' any more o' this Mr. O'Donoghue. You call me Seamus and we'll be the best o' friends. Now, there's not a lot of what you might call choice in these parts, apart from some ole cottages that won't do for a lady like yersel'. I was lucky t' get this. It's got fine stablin' and a paddock for the horses. Y' got good wood underfoot, not dirt like most places, and th' windows is glass. You'll be glad of it as the winter comes in. I grant it isn't exackly what a lovely colleen like you is used to, but w' a bit o' fixin up you'll be all right here."

At this point, Brigid came into the room to give the rabbit stew a stir. "Mr. O'Donoghue, sir," she said. "I tought that were your trap outside. Can I give y' somethin' t' keep the chill out?"

"I offered him a cup of tea," Brigid, "But he refused it."

"Och, Bridie knows what a man needs, don't y' Bridie?"

Brigid smiled and disappeared back into the scullery, coming back with a green glass bottle and a pewter mug.

"What's that?

"That's the *poitìn*, m'dear," said Seamus. "Ask no questions, and ye'll get told no lies. What the taxman don't see he don't grieve over."

"You mean it's illegal liquor?'

"Whisht! And if 'tis, who made it so? When the eejits in London said a man with a five hundred gallon pot had to pay tax on over tirty thousand gallons a month whether he made it or not, did they tink we were goin' to say yessir and pay? Sure and they can blame themselves if the pots went where no taxman can find 'em."

Lyla gave up. Between finding out that the locals might burn you for a witch and the housekeeper thought nothing of keeping illegal liquor in the scullery, she truly understood that she was no longer in the peaceable county of Middlesex. She also knew why her father's agent was no longer doing a good job. He was a drinker.

Chapter Ten

By the end of the first month, the group had settled into life in Newbridge or new bridge, whatever it should be called. The little family had been enlarged by the addition of a mother cat and two kittens and a good deal more furniture. When Lyla again impressed on Seamus the need for somewhere to put their things, he had Padraig drive her and Potter in his old carriage back to Dublin, where they had visited a furniture warehouse.

With all the building going on in the city, they were doing a roaring business. In their rather depleted stocks, Lyla was lucky to find two armchairs she and Potter could draw up to the fire, together with a linen press, a couple of candle stands, a washstand with a jug, bowl and waste water vessel, an armoire and a cabinet for her china. They were all in a rather more ornate continental style than she could have wished, but definitely better than nothing. She bought a pair of pretty French oil lamps that took her fancy. They featured frolicking nymphs and shepherds in a pastoral scene that was so far from the reality of the local countryside that they made her laugh. She also found a large gold framed mirror, also probably French.

She asked about carpets and curtains and was directed to a drapers. There they found two Turkish rugs, somewhat worn but still glowing with jewel tones, and a quantity of wine-colored velvet that a wealthy customer had ordered but disliking the color, had refused to buy. The furniture warehouse manager, charmed by Lyla's youth and her smile, agreed to have the lot delivered to her in Newbridge within the next week. Yes, he knew where it was, on account of the garrison.

The items duly arrived. When the carpets were unrolled, one under the beds and one under the table, the armchairs installed and the other furniture placed in appropriate spots around the room, the dwelling took on a completely different appearance. They put one of the pretty French lamps on a stand between their beds and the second on the dining table, whose scarred surface was covered with one of the lace tablecloths forming part of Lyla's mother's collection. Over the next week, Potter made curtains of the wine velvet and cushions for their dining chairs with the leftover pieces. Jeb hung the curtains floor to ceiling at the sleeping end of the room, so they had both privacy and the sense they were not sleeping and living all in one space.

When, on Lyla's instructions, Jeb hung the large gold mirror on the wall under the high windows, she laughingly declared, "Good thing we were not obliged to hang our undergarments on the hooks, because between that and the Continental furniture, it would look like those places my father and his cronies would talk about when they had forgotten I was there. From the tone of their voices I gathered they were not quite the thing."

"Miss Lyla!" said a horrified Potter, "I wonder your father let you stay when men were engaged in such talk!"

"Oh, I was a fixture, like one of the horses. No one ever noticed me. I learned some very interesting things that way!"

Potter shook her head in dismay, but Jeb, who hadn't understood what she'd said, looked around in wonder. "It's like magic, Miss," he said. "Like you waved a wand an' it all changed!"

"Shh!" Lyla giggled. "We don't want the folks hereabouts thinking we're witches. Didn't you hear what Mr. O'Donoghue said?"

Unmentionable establishment or not, the house was infinitely more comfortable with these changes. When the candlelight glowed against the ornate wooden furniture and velvet draperies of an evening, it looked cozy and homelike. The kittens certainly thought so. Once they were weaned, their mother returned to her old home. They did not appear to feel her loss; on the contrary, they set themselves up as masters of the domain. One of them would position himself behind the door to the scullery and wait for the ladies to pass through, whereupon he would leap up and hold onto the fringed ends of their shawls. Potter shrieked at the first unexpected attack.

"You little sneak!" she cried. So Sneak he became.

The other appeared to think his ancestors had been birds. He would all but fly to the highest places in the house: the top of the china cabinet in the parlor, the curtain in the bedroom and the dish rack in the scullery. From there he would survey the world beneath, occasionally, just for fun, reaching out a paw to catch at the ladies' caps. In the evenings he would leap up onto the back of one of the chairs and launch himself at the shoulders of whoever was sitting there.

"Sure and he's a rascal, that one," said Brigid. So Rascal it was.

The two cats quickly laid claim to the two fireside chairs. They would each jump onto one and give themselves elaborate tongue baths before falling asleep, Sneak against the cushions and Rascal along the back of the chair, hanging like a fur draped over a woman's shoulders. Potter, much less soft-hearted than her mistress where animals were concerned, would push one or the other off unceremoniously when she wanted to sit down herself.

"Oh no!" Lyla would cry. "They deserve a rest too! They work so hard!"

This was true. Most mornings there was a row of their victims neatly laid out in the scullery for Brigid's appreciation.

All this work went some way to taking Lyla's mind off Harry. He was still her first thought in the morning and the last at night and his much folded and re-folded letter was still taken out of her reticule and re-read, but during the day she sometimes found she hadn't thought about him at all for whole hours at a time.

She no longer worried about Jeb, having found out from Brigid that he took himself off of an evening to one or other of the inns up the road. It seemed they were split decisively between those for the locals and those for the British soldiers. Jeb, being neither, seemed able to pass between the two, and was to be found either with Padraig or with the enlisted men who were about his age. In no time he was well known not only to the locals but also to the off-duty soldiers.

It was through Jeb that the enlisted men, then the officers in the garrison, and through them their wives, became aware of the young lady and her companion newly arrived in the neighborhood. They began to receive afternoon calls from the ladies who lived within the walls of the garrison.

Chapter Eleven

The ranking officer in the garrison, which housed a company of the 3rd Light Dragoons called The King's Men, was a Lieutenant Colonel named Hutchings. According to convention, it was his lady who came first. She was a stern matron with a hooked nose who had spent her married life following her husband from one place to another and now, at the zenith of her power, felt herself as much in command as he. She confessed herself astonished to find such a young lady and with no one but her companion (for thus had Lyla introduced Potter to Brigid and word got around) living in such an out-of-the-way place, and moreover, in what amounted to a men's dormitory!

"My dear Miss Worsley," she said, "one wonders that your father should have allowed such a thing. It would have been impossible in my day." Her implication was that it should be impossible in any day.

"Oh," replied Lyla airily, determined to reveal nothing of the reason for her leaving home, "I have been involved in my Papa's business for so long, I don't believe he sees me as a female at all. Mr. O'Donoghue needs help, and here I am." Then, wishing to change the subject, "But tell me, Mrs. Hutchings, do the married officers live in barracks like these?" She gestured to her surroundings.

"Certainly not! The officers' quarters are proper homes. That is to say, they are townhomes, each with its own front door with a drawing room, dining room and necessary offices on the ground floor, bedchambers upstairs and servants' quarters above. The Lieutenant Colonel and I, of course, have a proper house in its own grounds."

"Oh," said Lyla, unable to think of anything to add.

But the Lt. Colonel's lady was more accustomed to speaking than to listening and continued without pause. "We are only in one place for a year or two, of course, but as wife of the Commanding Officer I do what I can to create a society wherever we are posted. We must not allow our standards to drop. We have musical evenings, card suppers and lectures. You will be a most valued addition, dear Miss Worsley! And you must not think we engage in nothing but frivolity. I have formed a literature society and a Christian Women's Guild to rescue fallen women. You must have seen that encampment?"

Lyla had remarked upon a ragged collection of tents that sprawled along the far wall of the garrison when she was riding with Seamus early after their arrival.

"'Tis the camp followers, me darlin'," he had said. "Sure and anywhere there's soldiers there's women to service their needs."

"Needs?" Lyla didn't immediately follow.

"Yes, of a personal nature, y'understand."

"Oh, yes, I see."

Then when she saw a young woman give Seamus a small wave, and him nod back, she thought the soldiers weren't the only ones whose needs were serviced.

But Lyla didn't want to be involved in any Christian Women's Guild to deal with the camp followers. Live and let live, was her motto.

"I'm afraid I won't have a great deal of time for your groups, excellent though I'm sure they are," she said now. "I really am here to help Mr. O'Donoghue. I anticipate being frequently from home at horse fairs. My father is counting on me."

"But surely you don't mean to do the actual buying yourself? With all those dirty men? Scoundrels, a lot of them are."

"Yes, I'm afraid I do. Mr. O'Donoghue can no longer walk around the fairs; his legs aren't what they were. But he'll know who the scoundrels are."

"If he isn't one himself," said her visitor, darkly.

After the visit of the Lt. Colonel's lady, the other wives appeared in descending order of rank, a fact which, when Lyla realized it, made her chuckle. The spouses of two Majors, four Captains and six Lieutenants appeared in due course. Three wives of Second-Lieutenants were the last to show up. They were the youngest and least experienced of the lot and evidently believed there was strength in numbers, as they came in a group.

When she asked whether other officers were married, a pretty, peaches and cream girl who looked younger than Lyla herself, answered, "Oh yes, but their wives stayed at home. Not many of us are able to come with our husbands, and nearly none with children. And of course, some are bachelors."

"A number of our men are away in Ballinrobe, dealing with the problems," added another of the group. "They're sadly missed." She sighed.

"Problems?" asked Lyla.

"Yes. I don't know what it's all about but the people don't seem to want us here. We don't understand it." She looked for support from her friends, who all shook their heads.

Lyla remembered that Jeb had reported the British soldiers weren't popular with the locals, and now it seemed in some places there was open revolt. It occurred to her for the first time that the British, including herself, were invaders in this land.

Over the next couple of months Lyla found herself invited to soirées in the garrison. She ate mediocre food, listened to mediocre musical entertainments from the warbling soprano of one of the officers' wives, to a clearly unhappy subaltern playing the pianoforte, and engaged in mediocre conversation with ladies obviously afraid to voice any opinion other than that of their Commanding Officer's wife. She was not unhappy to learn that they were to be replaced in December. A company of the 2nd Dragoons, called the Queen's Bays were coming, so named because they rode only bay horses.

Chapter Twelve

By then Lyla was busy with the business that had brought her there. As soon as they were settled in, Lyla began to urge Seamus to take her to the horse fairs. Like her father, he shook his head and said sure and he didn't think a young colleen like her would be able to deal with the rough men doing business there.

"Rubbish!" she replied stoutly. "They know you, don't they? If you say I'm working with you, they will treat me the same as they treat you. I can help you just as I helped my father. A woman can choose a horse as well as a man. We're not as weak as you think! Look at Brigid! She works all day here and still has her family's meal on the table. And I've seen her give that big son of hers a clout around the ear more than once. Besides, Jeb will come with me. He's not very large, but he's a fighter."

Jeb had indeed proven his mettle. The flow of young officers to her door predicted by Seamus had proved a reality. Most of them merely bowed and looked at her in adoration. Now and then one attempted to take her hand, and a couple of the more enterprising gave her a poem or a posy. But the lack of privacy in the one-room dwelling and the ever-present stern-faced Potter acted as an effective deterrent to anything further, and nothing ever came of these muted outpourings of love.

On one occasion, however, as Lyla was walking Firefly to the stables, a young officer emboldened by more ale than was good for him, surprised her by appearing round the corner, taking her by the waist and attempting to kiss her. In a flash, Jeb was at her side, tearing the unfortunate man's arm from around her and delivering an uppercut to his chin that sent him sprawling into the midden. He rose groggily to his feet and came forward in a classic fighting pose, but Jeb defeated him with a lightning fast one-two punch before he had a chance to strike a blow. He fell back again and this time didn't move.

"Goodness, Jeb," said Lyla. "I never took you for a boxer."

"I ain't Miss, but I got two older brothers and yer either learned fast or yer never got no dinner." Then, as she looked at the motionless form still lying in the muck, he said, "Don't you worry 'bout 'im. I'll get a couple of 'is mates from the boozer an' they'll get 'im 'ome."

Lyla learned afterwards that the young man had been stopped in his soiled uniform by a superior officer who learned first about the fight then the reason for it. He was confined to barracks for a month and reduced in rank. After that, approaches to Lyla became much more circumspect.

The first Irish fair Lyla attended was at Banagher, about 26 miles from Newbridge. It was there the British Army bought many of their horses. Lyla, Jeb and Seamus set out together, she riding Firefly, Jeb a rangy mare Seamus had provided and Seamus himself on a big old shire horse, the only breed that could take his weight. Their progress was not rapid, as Seamus favored an amble, or at most a trot. They had set out at sunrise but having stopped to bait at breakfast time, which for Seamus meant downing several tankards of ale, it was already mid-morning by the time they arrived at the fair.

Lyla was immediately carried back to the numerous such events she had attended with her father. The minute her nose smelled that special mixture of cigars and animal excrement, her pulse quickened. She was impatient to begin.

They left their horses in a paddock where for the price of tuppence, one of the lads promised to feed, water and watch them, then she turned to the agent.

"How do you want to do this, Seamus?" she asked, eager to be in the hunt.

"Well, alanna, first tings first, a man's got to clear the dust o'th'road from his gullet, so he has. You an' the lad wait here. Oi'll be back afore you know it."

"By no means! I'm not wasting time standing around. Tell me where you'll be and I'll find you when I've made some choices."

Seamus shrugged. "Sure an' I'll be at Feeney's. Ask anyone," he replied, and with that, he left them.

Lyla started off into the middle of it all with Jeb a few steps behind her, not sure where to begin. At home she and her father had bought for years from the same dealers, but here she knew no one. She realized she should have asked Seamus who he usually dealt with and where they could be found. She started back to find him, but as she came to the edges of the crowd, she saw a fine bay being led in. She could see no straw in its bridle, which, she knew, indicated it was not sold. She went straight up to the man leading it and asked the price.

"Fitty pound and no' a penny less," he answered.

He was an indescribably dirty, thin-faced individual with a strong odor. Lyla stood way back.

"I'll give you thirty."

"Forty-foive."

"Thirty-five."

"Forty."

"Done."

Then she realized she'd no money with her. Seamus had told her he'd bring the necessary, as he put it, and it was better she not carry cash on her person, especially not in a reticule, which could easily be snatched.

"Right. Stay here. I'll be back directly. Where's Feeney's?"

He signaled over to where a row of grey tents flapped in the breeze. Lyla almost ran through the crowd and after an exasperating search found Seamus leaning against a tall table laden with bottles.

"I need some money," she gasped, out of breath.

"Ay, alanna," he chuckled "Sure an' Oi've never met a woman who didn't!"

"Don't be idiotic!" Lyla was in no mood for his jokes. "I've found a horse and need to pay for it."

Mumbling something she couldn't catch, Seamus handed her a roll of notes. "Here," he said. "Hoide this in yer buzum."

"I most certainly will not," she retorted. She was wearing a button-up woolen cloak over a serviceable dress with deep pockets. It would be very difficult for anyone to steal the money from those.

She got back to the bay horse just in time to see a tallish man in well-fitting tweeds and a cap laughing and slapping the hand of its disreputable owner. He was better dressed than most of the other men at the fair. He took the bay's bridle and seemed about to lead it away .

"Stop!" shouted Lyla. "I agreed to buy that horse a few minutes ago! You can't steal it from under me!"

The man turned and faced her with a look of surprise. He had a pleasant, open face with bright blue eyes. The hair under his cap was dark and curly.

"So you're the lady Mick was telling me about," he said, speaking with just a trace of an Irish accent. "He told me a lady said she'd buy the horse but darted off without sealing the bargain. He didn't know what to make of it. Too late now, I'm afraid. The horse is mine."

"But we made a deal!"

"Did you slap hands?"

"Slap hands?"

"Yes, that's how you seal a bargain here, didn't you know?"

"No, I didn't." Lyla hadn't even considered getting within arm's length of the smelly individual, let alone touching him. "But he knew I wanted it and I was just getting the money."

"No, he didn't know what to make of it. Saying you wanted the horse but not slapping and not having any money. And it was nearly half an hour ago. He thought you might be a bit touched in the head, to tell you the truth. We were just laughing about it."

Lyla was enraged. "Laughing? At me? How dare he, and how dare you? Touched in the head indeed! I was simply not aware of the local custom of hand-slapping and I'd forgotten my agent told me not to carry money because of thieves. I had to go and get some. I've got the payment now, so I'll thank you to hand over the horse."

"Sorry, can't be done. Mick made an agreement with me, not you. He can't take your money now. Word would get around and no one would trust him."

"Then I'll buy the horse from you. Here, I have the money." She thrust it at him.

The man shook his head. "He isn't for sale."

"You don't mean to tell me you plan to keep him?"

"Yes, I do. It's how we do business here. Besides, he's just what I was looking for."

"You are standing there and telling me that although you know I was ahead of you and agreed in good faith to buy that horse, you don't intend to let me have it? You, sir, are no gentleman."

He smiled. "If you say so. But as I say, we have traditions here. I'm Finn Gallagher and I'm owner of this fine horse."

"Well, I hope to have no further acquaintance with you, Mr. Gallagher."

"In that case, good day, Ma'am." He gave her another charming smile, briefly lifted his cap, clicked up the horse and led it away.

Lyla watched him go in utter astonishment. She had never been treated like that in her life. Why, he had acted just as if she were… a man! She didn't know whether she was angrier with him or with herself for not appreciating that she had finally got what she had always wanted.

Chapter Thirteen

Lyla stamped her way back to Seamus, Jeb still behind her.

"Why, alanna, back already? And were ye about gettin' the nag?"

"No. I was too late. It was sold to someone else." She glared at Jeb, daring him to say a word, and then continued angrily, "You are not forgetting, I hope, Mr. O'Donoghue, that you are my father's agent. I represent my father. You therefore work for me and I expect you to do what you are paid for. Now, you will stop drinking and introduce me to the men you usually deal with."

Seamus looked at her but quailed before the fierce look in her eye.

"A man has t'quench his tirst, darlin', so he does. But sure and I'm ready if you are."

He led them away from the tents and around the field, introducing her to five or six dealers, all of whom hailed him with friendship and her with a nod. Seamus introduced her as Miss Worsley from England but gave no explanation as to her presence. They were clearly not accustomed to dealing with women buyers, and if she spoke they answered her questions either looking at Seamus or mumbling at their feet. The story was the same everywhere. Sure and it was a pity he hadn't come earlier! They'd had five or six fine animals, but hadn't they had to sell while they could. Lyla very quickly saw this was the reason for the poor stock they'd recently received back home.

In the end they were only able to purchase a big hunter and two pretty ponies, always the sort of thing popular for the children. It wasn't a very good day's work, and Lyla was still seething about the bay she'd lost.

Jeb took the horses to the paddock where they'd left their own mounts earlier in the day. By mid-afternoon it was full of men and boys preparing to leave. Amongst them, Lyla saw the man who'd bought the bay.

"What can you tell me about that man over there?" she asked Seamus, indicating the man in tweeds and a cap.

"Finn Gallagher?" replied the agent, following her look. "Squoire's youngest. Good man. Got a good eye fer a horse, he has. Sells 'em to t' army. Noice little bidness."

"Indeed!"

That information infuriated Lyla all over again. So he *was* going to sell that bay. But he wouldn't sell it to her! She looked at the other horses he'd assembled. Seamus was right. He did have a good eye. Well, so did she, and she would die before she'd let him get the better of her again!

By now Jeb had tethered the horses to their mounts for the ride home. He took the hunter and put one of the ponies each with Lyla and Seamus.

"I reckon that'll work, Miss Lyla," he said. "The pony ain't likely to take off with Mr. Seamus like the 'unter might. I won't say 'e's drunk as a wheelbarrow, but nigh on it!"

"Yes, I know he's been dipping rather deep, as the saying goes. We'll have to try to keep him away from any more until we get home."

This proved a hopeless case. They had to stop to rest and water the horses, whereupon Seamus immediately disappeared into the inn's taproom and had to be almost dragged out. It was dark by the time the garrison came into view. To do him credit, Seamus helped them stable the horses and carry hay and water into the stalls before taking himself off in the direction not of home, Lyla surmised, but of the nearest pub.

The following month the trio went to a much bigger horse fair in Ballinasloe. Being over 90 miles away, this required three days on the road, with two overnight stops. Back home Lyla probably would have been forced to take Potter or some other female with her, but here she hoped a well-known avuncular figure like Mr. O'Donoghue would be enough to give her countenance. No one could mistake him for any sort of lover. His boisterous humor could be heard in the taproom long after she had retired for the night and his roar when she went into his bedchamber early the following morning and poured a jug of water over his head to wake him up was by no means an expression of desire, except that of seeing her *go to the divil.*

But by dint of limiting Seamus's drinking time, Lyla got them all to the Ballinasloe fair before the day was far advanced. She would not let him get anywhere near the tents where the barrels of beer, porter and probably *poitín* were set up. He grumbled and shook his head like a bear, but she fixed him with her eye and made him take her around to his usual contacts. The dealers weren't inclined to pay any attention to her until they realized it was she who held the money and she who was driving the bargain.

Early in the day they were presented with a good-looking chestnut. Lyla noticed immediately that the animal's coat was shining, not from health but from being damp. He had obviously just been rubbed down. She asked to see him walk around and was suspicious when one of the owner's lads walked very close to its right hand foreleg. She observed closely and saw the animal was very slightly dragging its right hoof. The hoof wall had a square, beveled and polished appearance.

"The animal has a stifle joint problem that someone has tried to hide," she said. "He must have been sweating before you brought him round and he'll be totally lame if you continue to work him. I recommend you rest him for at least a month. I can write down the receipt for a good liniment if you like."

Seamus said nothing, but she saw a look pass between him and the dealer.

"Aye, alanna, you're right, so y'are," he said. "Sure and Joe were just playin' wit you."

"It's no problem for me, but I hope they'll look after the poor horse," she responded. "Here, this is what we use back home." She scribbled down a list of ingredients for a liniment. "You should be able to get these oils. Be careful with the oil of vitriol. But I'm sure you know that!"

Good humor was restored all round. Lyla never knew whether that had been a test or if they had genuinely tried to sell her a defective animal. Whatever it was, it never happened again and word must have spread, for thereafter the men dealt with her as readily as with Seamus. In the end, they were able to buy six good horses. Only then did Lyla release her agent with the instructions to be at the paddock by three that afternoon. She would leave, with or without him, and take his horse. So unless he wanted to walk home, he'd better be there.

She saw Mr. Gallagher's tweed cap a few times in the distance, but kept well away from him. She was pleased with her own purchases and had no desire to be involved with him. Jeb showed an inclination to stick protectively to her side, but once they found a tent where other women were sitting and where the only beverage offered was tea, she encouraged him to go and take a look around. Since the last thing he wanted to do was drink tea with his mistress, he gladly took himself off to watch the horse lunging contests and the wild, no-holds barred bareback races that were a side feature of the fair.

Chapter Fourteen

Lyla was sitting there enjoying her tea and watching the world go by when a familiar figure came into view and, with a lift of his cap, sat himself down in the chair opposite her.

"Miss Worsley," said her visitor. "Nice to see you again."

"I wish I could say the same, Mr. Gallagher," countered Lyla. "I've no wish to see you at all. But how is it that you know my name? I do not recall my having given it to you."

"You didn't, but when a beautiful young lady is ahead of me at every step and buys the very horses I would have bought myself, it's hard for me not to ask her name."

"Did I?" Lyla was so pleased at the second part of this remark, she ignored the first.

"You most certainly did. Though how you got old Seamus up to snuff is beyond me."

"I dare say it is. But it's no more than you deserve."

"I reject that absolutely, but you notice I do not repine and demand you sell them to me after all."

"That is because you know you cannot. I was careful to slap hands this time, even though I find it a barbaric custom. A man or woman's word should be enough. It is at home."

Finn Gallagher laughed. "But here, you must know, it's different. What a man says may just be the Blarney speaking. Words are just... words. A hand slap is undeniable."

By now Lyla had, of course, heard of the Blarney, and she had begun to understand that much of what she was told was usually more storytelling than fact. It certainly explained the hand slapping.

Gallagher smiled. "Anyway, it's no more barbaric than drinking tea at a horse fair. Please let me fetch you a glass of whisky. It'll do you a lot more good than that stuff. God knows what they put in it."

That hadn't occurred to Lyla, but now she looked at her tea suspiciously. "What do you mean?"

"It's made of plants and leaves, isn't it? Look around you. We have those and to spare. I shouldn't be surprised if it has oak and hay in it."

"And your whisky doesn't?"

"Of course not! We are very serious about it. Nothing but the purest ingredients. It's what keeps us going as a people and accounts for our good humor in the face of hardship. Now you stay here while I bring us some."

"I'm not required to slap your hand to prove I'll wait?"

"Now you're trying to beat me at my own game, Miss Worsley. But I know you English. Your word is your bond. I believe you'll be here when I return."

He strode off. Lyla was more than a little tempted to prove him wrong by leaving, but he was right. When a gentleman went to fetch something for you, you were honor bound to await his return. Besides, she was enjoying their banter. She hadn't had anyone to talk to since, well, since Harry, and he was of a more serious turn of mind. Finn Gallagher was full of the Blarney, just as he said his countrymen were. She couldn't help but like him, in spite of the business with the bay.

A few minutes later, he was back with two glasses of golden liquid, which he put on the table. Then from his pocket he produced a napkin with four *blaa* wrapped in it.

"These are fine" he said, sitting down. "Better than anything you can get in England." He took a huge bite of one.

Lyla had to agree. The *blaa* were soft and still a little warm. She experimented with a tiny taste of the whisky. The combination was delicious. She took another sip.

"There, what did I say? Better than tea any day!"

"It is very good," she admitted, "but I still think I'll stick mostly to tea. I don't want to end up like Seamus."

"Well now, he's a good man and knows his horses. But since his wife died a couple of years ago he's been hitting the bottle. I wondered how long it'd be before his English employers realized he wasn't fit for the job any more. 'Course, I didn't know they'd send a lady horse coper to brighten my day. Glad they did, though." He twinkled at her.

"My father didn't exactly send me. I asked to come."

"Why? Not enough fellers for you to dazzle in England?"

"Don't be silly. I wanted to come because…," she wasn't going to tell him the real reason, "… because I love horses and this is the best place to find them."

Finn didn't look convinced but he didn't press her.

They were silent for a moment, then Lyla asked, "How do you come to know so much about England?"

"My father sent me and my brother to Eton. He wanted us to understand the English. Most of my countrymen consider them the enemy." He saw her look surprised and added, "I'm exaggerating a little, but not much. But my family has always had good dealings with the English. My father sold the British Army the land the garrison is built on, you know. And the army has brought a lot of wealth into the area. Newbridge didn't really exist before."

"Yes, I found that out when I first got here."

"But we've also always traded with the French as well."

"Yes, I realized that when I saw all the French furniture in Dublin."

Finn nodded. "We're stuck in the middle, so to speak. Did you know Bonaparte bought his famous grey war horse here at Ballinsloe back in 1799? Named him Marengo after his triumph against the Austrians and rode him to all his victories in Europe. But the Russians captured his stables, including Marengo, in 1812 so when the horse appeared at Waterloo it wasn't with Napoleon on his back. Apparently he was capable of galloping for five hours straight. Now, there's a horse, for you!"

"Goodness, yes! Where is he now?"

"Somehow an English Baron got hold of him after Waterloo intending to put him to stud. He's in stables near Ely. But nothing has come of it, as far as I know. But he was wounded eight times on top of all those long gallops. Not many of us could sire children after all that!" he laughed.

Lyla wasn't used to gentlemen talking to her in such frank terms, and blushed.

"Excuse me," said Finn. "I get carried away on the subject of horses, I'm afraid."

"That's all right. I love them too. They work so hard for us and hardly ever get the thanks they deserve. I hope poor old Marengo is having a good life now." She looked at the watch pinned to her bosom. "Heavens! I have to get going. I was supposed to be meeting Seamus in the paddock at three and it's gone that now."

"Then I'll walk you over."

"There's no need," said Lyla, but when she got to her feet she found she was a little dizzy. She clutched the edge of the table.

"'Tis the whisky," smiled Finn, sounding very Irish all of a sudden. "Don't worry. You'll soon acquire a head for it!" He took her arm firmly under his own and guided her through the crowd.

When they got to the paddock, they found Jeb and Seamus waiting, the new horses already reined together.

"I don't doubt I'll be seeing you next month," said Finn as he took his leave. I've a mind to camp there overnight to get there before you."

"You wouldn't!"

"No! I wouldn't." He laughed at her dismay. "For sure it will be cold and raining and I like my bed as much as the next fellow. But I shall see you, Miss Worsley, and may the best man win!"

He lifted his cap, gave a slight bow and was gone.

Chapter Fifteen

Mr. Gallagher was absolutely right when he forecast bad weather for the next time they met. Lyla was glad she had listened to him and worn a heavy cloak with a hood. Seamus was all the more inclined to make for the refreshment tent first thing.

"Seamus," she said with steel in her voice, "if Mr. Gallagher steals all the good horses from under my nose because you have been remiss in introducing me to the best dealers, I shall dismiss you and write to my father to say I have done so. I would rather do business with your help, but I assure you I am quite prepared to do so without it!"

"Tush, now," replied the agent, "Sure an' Oi'll be showin' you how t'go on. But if it's Mr. Gallagher you'll be wanting to get ahead of, here he comes now. Will you be tinkin' o' hidin'?" He chuckled at his own humor.

Lyla scowled at him. Then, turning to Finn, who had reached them in a few long strides, "Good morning, Mr. Gallagher. Are you here to tell me I may as well go home because you've already bought everything worth having?"

"Good morning to you, Miss Worsley, though there's not much good about it. And is that what you think of me? That I'd be playing tricks on a lovely lady? No, Madam. On the contrary, I was wondering if you'd like to go around with me. We can work together instead of competing. It would be to your advantage because everyone knows me and wouldn't dare to try to rob you if I was standing there, and it would be to my advantage because they'll be so bedazzled by your beauty they'll forget what they're about." He smiled at her.

"And would my beauty be enough to dazzle *you* if we both wanted the same horse, Mr. Gallagher? Or is that just the Blarney again?"

He chuckled. "If we both want the same horse, we will come to an understanding." Then, changing his tone, he said seriously, "Look, this is the last fair of the year and they'll not be wanting to feed the animals over the winter. They'll want to sell, and sell fast. And no one wants either themselves or the animals standing around in this weather. Together we've got good bargaining power, better than in competition. What do you say?"

Lyla looked at him and at Seamus, who was already inching his way towards the tents. She knew if she went around with him, the agent would have his mind more on the bottle than on any purchases. "Very well, then, Mr. Gallagher. Let's give it a try. It will be interesting to see which of us tries to kill the other before it's over."

He chuckled again, tucking her hand under his arm. "Now, there are no circumstances on earth that would make me want to kill you, Miss Worsley, and killing me will be quite unnecessary. All you have to do is to say *Finn, my dear, my heart is set upon that horse* and I shall be as wax in your hands. You may have whatever you want."

"Just by calling you *my dear*?"

"And using my Christian name. It is the one spell that will work on all occasions."

Lyla laughed. "That is a good spell. I'll have to remember it."

They set off together, with Jeb as usual a few paces behind.

In the event, she didn't have to use the spell. It was as Finn had said. They were both able to buy what they wanted. Finn was always a gentleman, but he didn't coddle her the way Harry used to. If he was determined to have a horse, he said so, and she did the same. They were able to compromise as equals. It was a new experience for her, and she enjoyed it.

They were quickly done with their business, which was just as well, as the rain showed no sign of letting up and they were both soon drenched. They reined up all the horses and left as early as they could, Finn saying he would ride to Newbridge with them as he was going that way anyway. It was lucky he did, for Seamus had imbibed so freely that he was incapable of doing anything more than slump in his saddle. His horse, disliking the rain and the heavy going, went slower and slower and would have stopped altogether had Finn not taken the reins and forced it to maintain the same trot as the rest of the group.

It was pitch black by the time they got home, the moon hidden by a thick layer of clouds, and the rain still pouring down. They all set to work with gritted teeth, stabling and rubbing down the horses, including those belonging to Finn, who said he would put up at one of the inns for the night. The weather was too foul to continue. Brigid's husband and son came to give a hand, along with a lad called Nolan they'd engaged to help Jeb in the stables, and Seamus, who had finally woken up in the last hour or so. This was probably because his sodden hat no longer kept the rain from dripping down his neck. He had been too drunk to fully button his coat when they left and was now regretting it. Finn didn't try to persuade Lyla to go inside and let the men do the work as Harry would certainly have done. Instead they worked companionably side by side until the last horse was in a dry stall with clean straw, fed and watered.

Then Brigid shooed them all into the scullery, telling them to wash their hands at the sink, hang their wet cloaks on the pegs with which the dormitory was so plentifully provided, and get some hot soup into themselves before they all perished of the cold. She ordered her menfolk, Jeb and Nolan to dig into the enormous pot she'd put on the scullery table, and ushered Lyla, Seamus and Finn into the parlor. Potter had obviously been getting things ready. The fire glowed, the curtains were drawn, the candles were lit and the table was laid. The cats were curled up in the fireside chairs. Nothing could have looked more inviting.

"Potter, you know Seamus, and this is Mr. Gallagher," said Lyla briskly as they came in. "He has very kindly helped with the horses and he's going to have dinner with us. Mr. Gallagher, this is Miss Potter, my companion."

Finn bowed, "At your service, Miss Potter," he said. He looked around appreciatively but hung back, not taking off his cloak. "Who would have believed this place could be turned into such a comfy parlor? And no, I won't sit down in all my dirt. I can get something at a pub."

He bent to tickle Rascal behind the ear, and the cat pushed its knobby little head against his hand. Lyla thought if cats and horses liked a man, he must have a good heart.

"If you think you can leave without being fed, you don't know Brigid," she laughed. "Sit down for heaven's sake, both of you. I can't imagine why you are worried about your dirt. My skirt is more mud than wool!"

The men both sat and Potter served the soup. The office of serving a meal to guests, together with the entirely new experience of having a gentleman bow and assure her of his being at her service, made Potter acutely aware of how her situation had changed. Back at home, she would never have greeted visitors or sat at table with them. Seamus called for a bottle of *poitìn*, which even Potter was persuaded to try. Her normally sallow cheeks became quite pink. With Seamus's rowdy good humor and Finn's endless stories, it was the most convivial evening they had spent since they arrived.

The visitors finally rose to take their leave. Seamus went into the scullery to have a word with Brigid about the *poitìn* supply, Lyla suspected, and Finn said his goodbyes. The cats had both left their cushions during the meal, each in turn trying to jump on his lap, a thing they were never normally allowed to do when the ladies were at table. Now they were wreathing around his ankles. He bowed again to Potter and pressed Lyla's hand.

"'Tis a pity that was the last fair until the spring," he said. "We make a good team. But no doubt I'll be seeing you, Miss Worsley. I'm often in these parts. I do a deal of business with the garrison next door."

"The cats will be glad to see you," she replied.

"And I'll be glad to see them, though not as glad as I shall be to see the other inhabitants of the home," he replied with a grin.

"Well," said Potter when he left, "what a charming gentleman!"

"Don't tell me you were taken in by his Blarney," commented Lyla. "But I have to admit, he's got a way with horses and cats."

But even as she said it, she knew she was being churlish. She liked him too. It wasn't just that he treated her as an equal, she enjoyed his company, and there was no denying his charm.

Potter nodded, but tidied away the dinner things thinking it wasn't only horses and cats Finn Gallagher had a way with. And as Lyla lay in bed that night, her last thoughts were not, as they usually were, of Harry, but of Finn.

Chapter Sixteen

Lyla's father had been very pleased with the horses they had sent so far, writing in a note that they'd all sold at good prices, especially the hunters. He commented that Seamus must be quite his old self. She didn't disillusion him, feeling sorry for the old man who'd lost his wife and realizing that although she didn't need him for the fairs, she did need his experience in other aspects of the business, particularly in the paperwork and practicality of shipping the animals. He had two reliable lads who sailed with the horses from Dublin to Liverpool, where they were met by counterparts from her father's stables.

She wanted to send over the last group of horses as soon as possible. With the winter drawing in, the crossing would become increasingly difficult. But horses, like people, need time to settle down in one place before being shipped somewhere else, especially if the trip is liable to be traumatic. Lyla and Jeb therefore spent the next weeks exercising the animals and making sure they were in top physical condition for the crossing that was bound to terrify them.

She was riding Firefly a few days after the last group of horses had been dispatched to her father, feeling at a loose end, and, in spite of herself, wondering what Finn was doing, when, as if by magic, she saw the man himself coming towards her. He was leading a row of bays. Amongst them was the horse she had tried to buy.

"I suppose you're on your way to sell that bay," she said, feeling a little awkward.

"And good morning to you, Miss Worsley." He grinned. "Yes, I've been keeping him until the 2nd Dragoons were installed in the garrison. They'll pay well for a good-looking bay. They aren't called the Queen's Bays for nothing! But he can still be yours. You know the spell."

"You wouldn't sell him to me before and If you think I'm going to utter those words now for the sake of a horse, or anything else, you don't know me," she retorted.

He laughed. "I know you better than you think! Why else would I risk losing a fine animal that the colonel himself might take a shine to?" and he resumed his trot up towards the garrison gate.

She watched his back, still half resentful at having lost the horse, but somehow pleased he hadn't given in to her. She sighed, then set about her own day's work.

The afternoon was just beginning to darken into evening and Lyla was behind the drapery of the bedroom changing out of her riding dress for dinner, when a knock came at the door. She heard Potter's delighted, "Oh! Mr. Gallagher, do come in!" followed by meows of welcome from the two cats.

"I was just passing by and thought I'd pay my respects to you, Miss Potter," came the reply.

"To me?" Potter was astonished. Never in her life had a personable gentleman evinced the slightest desire to pay her his respects.

"Yes, I spoke to Miss Worsley this morning, but I haven't had the pleasure of seeing you since that delightful evening here. I hope you are well?"

"Yes, indeed! But please won't you sit by the fire? It's so cold outside!"

"Thank you! For the pleasure of your company, I will, Miss Potter. But just for a moment. I've an hour's ride back."

Then Potter's voice came in a different tone. "No, Rascal! Don't catch at Mr. Gallagher's coat like that! I'm sorry, sir, he always sits on the back of the chair waiting for a victim!"

"I don't think anyone could describe Mr. Gallagher as a victim," announced Lyla, emerging from behind the curtain.

"Miss Worsley!" Finn stood and turned with Rascal over his arm hanging limply like a piece of wet linen, "Lo! You appear like a goddess from behind the arras!"

She couldn't help laughing. "I believe you've mixed your images. The goddess rose from the sea, on a shell, as I remember, and the arras is used by people to hide behind when they wish to overhear conversations."

"And were you wishing to overhear mine with Miss Potter? She was kindly saving me from this ferocious animal." He indicated the cat, completely relaxed over his arm.

"Certainly not! I was…," she suddenly realized she didn't at all want to give their visitor an image of her changing her clothing. "I… I'm glad you know what a risk you are running sitting in the chair Rascal regards as his own. My caps are all in shreds."

"Then my sympathy is entirely with him. You should not be wearing caps at all!"

"As I've told her, again and again, Mr. Gallagher!" cried Potter. "As young and pretty as she is. It's bad enough she's stuck here with no company without making herself out to be a spinster!"

"No company? Then my mission here comes at a good moment. I happened to mention I would be coming past and Mrs. Amahlia

Beaufort, the new colonel's lady, asked me to drop off this invitation to a ball to mark the 2nd Dragoons installation here. If the jewels she was wearing are anything to go by, it's bound to be a glittering affair."

"So you didn't come to pay your respects to Miss Potter, after all!"

"Aha! You *were* listening behind the arras! And to be sure I did. She's included in the invitation. I was just about to present it to her when you appeared and I was struck dumb by your beauty."

"Mr. Gallagher, you are outrageous! I've a mind to show you the door!"

"No, Miss Lyla!" cried Potter, "The poor man's going to have a cup of tea! He's got a long ride home in the cold."

"The poor man doesn't like tea," said Lyla. "According to him, it's made of leaves and twigs. I don't doubt he'd rather have some of that illegal stuff Brigid keeps in the scullery."

And indeed, Brigid must have heard the sound of his voice, for there she was with the green bottle and three glasses.

"I heard you were in these parts, Mr. Gallagher, sir," she said. "Will ye be after stoppin' to take a bite w' the ladies? I've a lovely pie joost ready."

As strange as it was to hear the housekeeper inviting guests to dinner, Lyla added her voice to that of Potter in encouraging Finn to stay. She really was glad to see him and anyway, she wanted to hear more about the ball.

"Yes, please stay, Mr. Gallagher," she said. "We're feeling very flat after all the to-do getting the horses off."

"Then I gratefully accept," he replied with a smile. "Brigid's pies are famous, and the company," he bowed at all three women, "is the best in the county."

Chapter Seventeen

Lyla duly replied to the invitation to the Installation Ball, though she had a hard job persuading Potter that she should go.

"But Miss Lyla, I've never been to a ball in my life," she cried. "I can't dance and indeed I don't want to! My father was formal in forbidding it, as you know, and I would find it an affront to his memory. Besides, I've nothing to wear!"

Lyla did know that Mr. Potter, of blessed memory, had been a strict Methodist and deplored both dancing and music. But Lyla had foreseen this problem.

"Potter, dear, I replied to the invitation that as my duenna, you would naturally accompany me. Duennas are not expected to dance. You will sit with the mamas and watch. You know you'll enjoy that! And as for having nothing to wear, I'm sure we can do something with one of my evening gowns. I don't think a ballgown would be the thing, since you will not be dancing, but my amber silk will suit you very well. We are much of a height."

"Miss Lyla! Use one of your silk gowns, that I could not! Anyway, they would not fit! I'm so thin and you are, well…"

"I know!" Lyla laughed. "I'm *well endowed*! But we can take in the top a trifle. And that amber will look fine with your brown hair and eyes.

She would not take no for an answer, and thus it was that on the appointed day, the two ladies stood in front of the large gold framed mirror and beheld their reflection, the one with a shrug and the other with wonder. Lyla was wearing one of the ballgowns made for her London season. It was of a very pretty rose-colored silk that fell to her toes in soft folds from beneath her shapely bosom, ending in a short train, which she caught up on her wrist. It was embellished with silver floss around the bodice and hem, so that when she moved it flashed in the candlelight. Potter had threaded a pink ribbon through the brown curls caught on the top of her head, and round her neck she wore the silver locket with her mother's likeness inside.

"Oh, Miss Lyla, you do look lovely," sighed Potter. "You said you didn't want me to pack your ballgowns, but you must be glad I did."

Lyla shrugged. She didn't admire herself at all. She had always wished to be a little taller and, well, not quite so *well developed*. Her ideal was the tall, willowy damsels she had seen during her season in London. They looked as though a puff of wind would carry them off. She thought wryly that it would take a hurricane to lift her off her feet, and it would more than likely just drop her in the mud.

It had rained almost continuously the last few weeks and mud was the abiding element of their daily life. The road in front of their house was a quagmire, and the walk to the stables a wade in mud past their ankles. The hem of Lyla's riding dress had to be dried and brushed so ferociously every day that it had become a quite different color from the rest.

"In this weather, no one can look their best, so it's hardly worth trying," she replied. "But you look marvelous, Potter! I knew that amber would become you, and the lace is a triumph!"

It was true. Potter had been amazed when she looked at herself. As a lady's dresser, even one promoted to the role of companion, she usually wore nothing but grey and black, and her tidy but uninteresting gowns did nothing to enhance her thin figure. Now she couldn't believe the reflection that looked back at her. The rich color of the gown brought out the tints in her hair and skin in a way that the dull greys and blacks never did. It had been taken in to fit her narrow top, and Lyla had encouraged her to enhance the neckline with a deep ruffle of lace taken from the edges of one of her inherited tablecloths.

"Ruin one of your mother's linens?" Potter had cried. "That I will not do, Miss Lyla, not for a thousand balls!"

"It will not be ruined. You can hem the tablecloth up and no one will notice the difference. I would do it myself, but you know if I do, it will look like a bandage — covered with my blood from pricking myself, which I'm bound to do. It's my tablecloth and I'm ordering you to do it! I can't have my duenna looking shabby!"

In the end, Potter did as she was bid, putting a ruffle around the neck of the gown, and using the rest for the ends of the sleeves. She was accustomed to improving and embellishing her late ladyship's garments, and even Lyla's, when she would let her, but it had never occurred to her to do anything with her own. She had been thin and plain all her life. Her father had said that the good Lord had intended it to be so, and to go against His work was a sin. She should be satisfied as she was. But now, her bosom looking fuller by the addition of the ruffles, and her hair, which was usually braided into tight bands around her head, gathered loosely into a bun in the nape of her neck and gently waving, she didn't recognize herself. She was not beautiful, but she was elegant and she looked twenty years younger.

After a quick look at herself, Lyla had started to pace. The rain had at last stopped and Jeb had spread straw in front of the door, but now that it was upon her, she didn't really want to go to this ball. But Seamus would be there soon to collect them and she had accepted the invitation. It would be unmannerly not to show up.

"I hope Seamus doesn't drink so much he forgets to send the carriage," said Lyla, thinking nonetheless that it would be a good excuse to stay home. "I wouldn't put it past him."

But just at that moment a knock came at the door. The ladies gathered up their cloaks and Potter opened it — to reveal not Seamus or his driver, but Finn Gallagher. He was almost unrecognizable, wearing a dark cloak and tall hat in place of his habitual tweeds and cap. He looked very fine.

"Good heavens, Mr. Gallagher!" exclaimed Potter. "You are a welcome sight, sir."

"And you are a lovely sight, Miss Potter," he returned with a smile. "I know you for a comely woman, but this beauty dazzles me."

While Potter fluttered in confusion, he turned to Lyla. A different look came into his eyes as he looked at her, but all he said was, "Good evening, Miss Worsley. When I found out Seamus was supposed to be conveying you to the ball, I told him I would do it. That heavy old barge of his leaks like a sieve and would probably get stuck in the mud."

"Thank you, Mr. Gallagher, that is very kind," replied Lyla neutrally, though her heart had leaped when she saw him. *Don't be silly* she told herself. *It's just that he looks so different in evening clothes.*

She pulled her cloak around her shoulders and allowed herself to be led to his carriage, which was, indeed, a much newer and finer affair than the one they had travelled in from Dublin. Once she was safely inside, Finn returned for Potter, and the three of them set off the short distance to the Colonel's House, inside the garrison gate.

The evening turned out to be a much more glittering affair than Lyla had imagined. The battalion had only recently been sent to Ireland and the officers' wives had had the opportunity to purchase new garments before leaving. The result was a modish and even extravagant turnout. The shining Regimentals of the men and the elegance of many of the ladies would not have been out of place in a London ballroom.

She and Potter were presented to their hosts, whom they had never before met. The colonel's lady was wearing a sumptuous gown with a beaded bodice. It winked and shone in the blaze of the hundreds of candles with which the ballroom was lit. She had a headdress of plumes held by a flashing jeweled clasp. So large was it, that when she turned her head, the men in her vicinity had to step smartly back to avoid being dashed in the eyes.

"I couldn't believe it, my dear," she said to Lyla, swiping at Finn's breast with a large plumed fan matching her headdress, "when Finn here told me there was an English gentlewoman living in a sort of dormitory just next door." *So,* thought Lyla, *they are already on first name terms!* "In such a wild and lawless place, with no man to watch out for you! Well, you may be sure my men will keep an eye on you. Dear Queen Caroline allowed us to carry her name, you know, for our special attachment to her Majesty, and thus all ladies."

"That is exceedingly kind of you, Madam," replied Lyla, "but we have never felt threatened in any way by the local people. They have been nothing but kind and generous. In fact, the only time I have felt any alarm has been from soldiers within these walls."

The colonel's lady sucked in her breath. "Ah! The Thirds! The King's Own! I'm not surprised. But I assure you, you will have nothing of that kind from us. All my boys are gentlemen!"

In the short time since the new soldiers had moved in, there had been no reduction in the rowdy behavior in the pubs lining the street opposite the garrison and Lyla was inclined to think her hostess was prejudiced, but she said nothing. Other guests were by now lined up to greet their hosts, so Finn led them away to a sofa against the wall. He gently deposited Potter and said to Lyla, "I'd best come with you to procure a dance card so I may sign up for the waltzes right away, if there are any. But I have the feeling my lady colonel may have scruples against such a dashing dance."

Lyla's heart contracted at the idea of dancing a waltz with Finn. She told herself it was because the only man she had ever truly enjoyed waltzing with was Harry. When Finn turned out to be correct — the lady thought the waltz altogether too fast and permissive for her boys — she didn't know whether to be relieved or sorry.

Something must have shown on her face, for as he signed his name for the *Belle Assemblée* and a cotillion, Finn said, "Do you not care to waltz, Miss Worsley?"

"Oh, yes, I do! I... I mean, no. I should not want to waltz this evening."

He laughed. "That's a tangled answer!"

Lyla tried to brush it aside. "I mean, I'm out of practice and I fear I should step on the gentleman's toes."

Finn said softly, "I should be very surprised if any man objected to having his toes stepped on by you. I know I wouldn't."

Lyla looked up. His eyes were dark and inscrutable. "The Blarney again, Mr. Gallagher?"

"No, indeed. On my honor, nothing but the pure truth."

Chapter Eighteen

When Lyla looked back on the evening it was with very mixed feelings. The ball had resuscitated all the feelings of the Squire's May Ball where she'd seen Harry again after his travels. It seemed a lifetime ago. She'd gone there out of social obligation and had ended up falling in love. She'd waltzed with Harry, glad her aunt had made her take lessons, although at the time she had strenuously objected. She'd felt her feet had wings and her heart too. She never had that sensation again all the time she was in London, dancing with other men who were more handsome, richer and possibly more charming, if she'd ever listened to more than half of what they said.

But tonight she had enjoyed dancing. Her card had been filled almost immediately by men who all looked splendid in their regimentals. Apart from the normal banalities, not many of them appeared to have a great deal of conversation, but in the constant movement of the country dances one had nearly no time to talk with one's partner, so she felt no loss. Each pressed her hand meaningfully at the end and asked to be permitted to take her into supper, but Finn had already declared that was his prerogative.

Ah, Finn! He partnered her for the *Belle Assemblée*, the dance beginning the whole affair, as well as for the lengthy cotillion, and was at his most light-hearted. His blue eyes twinkled merrily and he talked engaging nonsense. And how handsome he was, even compared with the men in uniform. At the horse fairs in his tweeds and cap he looked fine, but at the ball, in black breeches with white hose, a well-cut swallow-tailed coat over a sober waistcoat and an elegant neckcloth held with a diamond pin, he looked wonderful. As she sailed around the floor with him, Lyla realized that for the first time since that awful moment in the Blankleys' garden, she was happy.

She saw other women's eyes following them jealously and couldn't help a feeling of triumph. He only danced with her twice, of course. He partnered other women: belles, wallflowers, and matrons, including the Colonel's lady. He made every one of them smile. When he caught her eye across the room, she smiled too, then blushed and looked down.

Potter was loud in her praise. "I have never met a more handsome and pleasant gentleman than Mr. Gallagher," she announced. "He even asked *me* to dance! Of course, I explained my scruples, which he readily accepted. Such good manners! He brought me some punch. It was delicious!"

Her companion was not given to exclamations of delight, and on the way home Lyla was surprised to hear Potter say suddenly, "This has been the most enjoyable night of my life, Mr. Gallagher, for which I know I have you to thank. I'm sure you mentioned me to the colonel's lady, or I would never have received an invitation. The gowns! The music! The collation! The delicious punch! All of the very first order. Thank you so very much."

"My dear Miss Potter," he responded. "It is I who should be thanking you. I entered the room with the two loveliest ladies on my arms and there was not a man there who didn't envy me. My credit in the world has risen enormously, I can tell you. They will be falling over themselves to buy my horses!"

"It was a lovely evening," agreed Lyla, "but I think I should draw your attention to the weather. It has begun to rain again in earnest. I can see that what we had before was just a prelude. How we are to get indoors without being soaked, I don't know. I wish we had our boots. Our shoes will be ruined."

"Leave it to me," said Finn, "though didn't you tell me Venus rose from the sea? You can surely rise from the mud!"

"More likely sink in it to my knees!"

But when they arrived in front of their home, Finn leaped out, telling them both to stay where they were. He wedged open the front door, then came back and before she had a chance to say or do anything, swept Potter up in his arms and carried her inside.

"Build up the fire, Miss Potter!" Lyla heard him say. Then he was back.

"You're not carrying me, Mr. Gallagher!" she said. "Potter is a lightweight, but I'm not!"

"You're the most delicious armful any man could ever carry," he replied, paying no attention whatsoever, and gathering her up. "I thank God for this rain!"

He held her close to his chest and looked down at her. The hard muscles beneath his cloak and the manly smell of him made her catch her breath. It seemed for a moment as if he might kiss her, but he did not. Instead, he swept her out of the carriage and into the house, where he deposited her on her feet.

Lyla found she was breathing fast, and was disappointed when she heard him say, "And now I shall wish you good night. I shouldn't keep the horses waiting any longer in this weather." He bowed and swiftly went back outside, closing the door behind him.

The two ladies looked at each other, both too shocked to speak. Lyla recovered first.

"Well!" she said. "What do you think of that?"

"I think," said her faithful companion slowly, "that my dear father will turn in his grave to hear me say it, but I think I should very much like a man to carry me indoors every day!" She sank down in one of the chairs, giggling and narrowly missing Sneak, who only scrambled out of the way just in time.

Lyla looked at her. Potter's cheeks were very pink. Then she remembered her companion had more than once mentioned the delicious punch. She smiled and shook her head. "I'm afraid the Blarney and the punch, which almost certainly contained a good measure of that *poitìn*, are affecting you most dreadfully. We'd better go back to England soon, before I come home and find you've joined the camp followers."

The two ladies prepared themselves for bed, carefully hanging up their fine dresses, Potter all the while gaily reviewing the evening with most uncharacteristic enthusiasm. She fell asleep almost immediately, but Lyla lay awake, warm in the happiness that still enveloped her. Then suddenly the reference to the camp followers came back into her mind. It was all very well to make a joke of it, but life must be very hard indeed for the women who were still living out there in the rain and cold. In the morning she would go and take a look.

Chapter Nineteen

The next day, poor Potter awoke with what she called *a head*. She blamed the endless rain that had for days prevented her from going for a good long walk. Lyla was sure it was the effects of the punch from the night before and hid a smile. She brought her a cup of tea and urged her to stay in bed.

Now she didn't have the horses to see to, she herself ate a leisurely breakfast and then put on her much-brushed riding dress.

"But you're not riding today, in this weather!" said Potter, wincing as she raised her head from the pillow.

"Believe it or not, it has actually stopped raining, and yes, I am going to exercise poor Firefly. He's probably suffering from being indoors just as much as you! Just try to sleep off your headache, Potter, dear. I'll ask Brigid to make us some broth for lunch. That will do you good."

"Make sure you take Jeb with you! Your father wouldn't approve of you riding off all alone amongst strangers!"

Lyla was forcibly reminded of Harry and smiled. "You know perfectly well he wouldn't give it a second thought! And the people around here aren't strangers! To them, I'm the mad Englishwoman, but they wave in the kindest fashion as I go by. You and I both know it's the drunken soldiers who cause the most trouble, but our colonel's lady assured us they're all gentlemen, so we've nothing to worry about!"

She pulled on her boots and strode outside. A weak sunshine had indeed replaced the rain, but it was still cold and damp. As she approached the stables, she saw Jeb talking to a young woman who barely came up to his armpit. Curls of flaming red hair were escaping from the shawl pulled tightly around her head and across her front. He seemed to be trying to persuade her of something. She shook her head and put her hand on his chest in an intimate fashion. When she approached, the girl bobbed a curtsey and ran off.

"A new friend, Jeb?" she asked.

"Y'could say that, Miss Lyla. She's Nolan's sister, Maeve."

Nolan was the lad they'd hired to help with the horses. Now the animals had been shipped off, there wasn't really enough work for both him and Jeb, but Lyla guessed that his family needed the lad's income and was reluctant to turn him off. So, while she was sure the young woman was more to Jeb than just Nolan's sister, she let that go, and said, "I've been meaning to talk to you about Nolan. Is there something we can have him do over the winter? I hate to just dismiss him."

To her surprise, Jeb looked down and then up at her, his face red. "Well, Miss, I've been thinkin' I'd like a bit more of a real place to live, like. Not that I'm not 'appy bedding down in the stable as 'tis, but if I was ever to... to want to settle down, I'd need... well... I'm lookin' fer a cottage or summat and he could 'elp me fix it up. 'E's a dab 'and with carpentry."

Lyla was astonished.

"You mean you want to settle down here? You don't want to go back to England?"

"No, Miss. I like it 'ere. I like th'... people.

So that was it. Jeb wanted to marry that girl and stay here forever. And she might have to stay here forever because she couldn't marry the man she wanted. How ironic. But she smiled.

"That sounds like a marvelous idea."

They walked companionably into the long stable where only Firefly, Jeb's horse Tinker, and a pony for the trap still stood, peacefully snuffling around in their stalls. Seeing her, Firefly nickered and put his head over the gate. She patted his long nose and gave him a piece of carrot, then because the other two sensed a treat was in the offing, gave them some too.

She walked to the end where the bridles and saddles were kept and made to lift down Firefly's, but Jeb was too quick for her.

"I'll do that, Miss Lyla," he said. "A lady like you shouldn't be liftin' that 'eavy stuff."

Lyla laughed. "You don't remember my father saying if you want to ride a horse you'd better be prepared to saddle one up. I think he was hoping to discourage me, but it didn't. I just did it, even when the saddle was almost as big as I was."

"Yes, Miss. All the blokes in the stable back 'ome reckoned as 'ow you could do it better'n all o' them. And quicker too." Then, in a different tone, "D'you miss it, Miss Lyla?"

"Yes, I do," she replied quietly. "But I couldn't stay and see...," she stopped, not wanting to continue.

Perhaps Jeb knew the reason for their departure. He'd been the one she'd flung Firefly's reins to when she galloped back from Blankley House that fateful day. In any case, he didn't question her further. Instead he said, "Well, I don't. There I were just one o' the lads. Saving yerself, Miss, I'm in charge here. I'm me own man."

"Yes, you are, Jeb. And no one could want a better one. Now, you go ahead and get your place built. You deserve it."

Chapter Twenty

Lyla rode at a steady trot to the other end of the garrison, thinking over what Jeb had said. The happiness of the night before was still lingering, but she knew she couldn't slough off the memory of home so easily. The view of Harry as he took the hand of a fiancée who wasn't her burned in her memory, and the letter he'd written her was falling to pieces from being read and re-read.

It was still not midmorning but the pubs opposite the garrison were in full swing. The "gentlemen" of the Queen's Bays evidently enjoyed a good time. She came around the end of the wall and on the vacant land that lay just beyond it beheld a sight that swept her own miseries from her mind. Dozens of sad-looking tents and lean-tos slumped there, some with the remains of a dead fire in front but others looking totally abandoned.

Just at that moment, a faint ray of sunlight pierced the clouds, making the place look worse, if anything, as the light fell on churned-up mud, sodden ashes, splattered tar-covered cloth and pieces of rough timber. As she watched, a woman clad apparently only in a shift and a shawl, her feet in clogs, came out of one of the tents with a chamber pot in her hand. She walked to the edge of the encampment and threw the contents onto a filthy pile hulking there. The midden, evidently.

The woman returned to her dwelling and a few minutes later, a soldier emerged, buttoning up his coat and calling out, "See yas, Eileen!" before stamping away.

Lyla slid down and tethered Firefly to a tree. The mud sucking at her boots, she made her way across to the tent the woman and soldier had emerged from. An overflowing water barrel stood next to it.

"Hello? Eileen?" she called. "May I speak to you?"

"Who's that?" a suspicious voice came from inside. "If yer from t' church, get away. I don't need the loikes of you."

"I'm not from the church. I just want to talk."

There was a sound from inside and the dank piece of fabric covering the entrance was pushed aside. The woman stood there. She was younger than Lyla had first thought, although her dirty, worn face and stringy hair made it impossible to say exactly how old she was. She had pulled a muddy skirt over her shift and her shawl was pulled tightly over her shoulders and across her thin body, with the ends tied around her waist.

"Who're you? And how are y' after knowing my name?" She looked Lyla up and down suspiciously.

"I'm Lyla Worsley, but I'm nobody. That is, nobody important. I heard the… gentleman who just left call you Eileen. That's how I know. I just wanted to see how you … well, you all were getting on in all this rain. And cold."

"Bloody awful. That's how we're getting' along. What's it t' do with you?"

"I wanted to see if I could help at all." She looked around helplessly, "But I don't know where to begin."

"Sure an' if yas got a load o' straw we could lay down over the mud, y'could begin with that."

"I don't, but I can try to get some. What else do you need?"

"Somewhere out o' the bloody rain where we can build a foire and make a cup o'tay an' dry out our traps. Whoile yer at it, build us a bloomin' castle, why don't ya?" She laughed sarcastically.

Lyla took a breath and asked, "May I look inside? So I can get a better idea of how you... you live?"

Eileen looked straight at her and must have seen something in her face that made her mutter, "Sure, an' welcome to me parlor." She pulled aside the filthy strip of cloth that served as a front door and stood aside while Lyla stepped in.

A fug of unwashed bodies hit her nose, and under it a faint stink of excrement. It was almost completely dark, and it took a minute of two for her eyes to adjust. The tent was held up by two rough poles. The ground was covered with some sort of platform. In the back it was strewn with a tumble of dirty bedlinen. In front, where she was standing, there were a couple of wooden boxes, one of which held a tankard, the remains of a pie and a stump of a candle stuck on a dirty, chipped plate. The only other thing in there was the chamber pot. It was no warmer than outside, but the place was surprisingly dry.

"How do you keep the rain out?" she asked.

"Canvas covered w' tar. Y' gets one of the men t' elp. Sure an' they don't want t'do it in the rain no more than you do. If they want t' 'ave a bit o' the other, they got to fix yer up. Always canvas and stuff layin' around inside there." She lifted her chin towards the garrison. "In th' spring 'n summer there's more o' us. A lot is woives of the men as can't get housin'."

"You mean some of the women are married to the soldiers but can't live in the barracks?"

"Yes. Most of 'em is, with their kids. Them in charge don't loike 'em to be married and they won't 'ave 'em inside. A lot of 'em leave when it gets too cold."

"Good heavens! I had no idea. I thought you were all... well, you know. I'm sorry. Are you married, Eileen?"

"Not bloody loikely! Oi seen enough o' that with me Mam. Knocked 'er about, did me Da. Not fer me!"

They were both quiet for a moment, then Lyla asked, "But those of you who stay, how do you manage? Where do you cook when it rains?"

Eileen laughed. "We don't bloody cook, that's where! Can't make no foire, can't even warm up a kettle o'water. Oi'd give me right leg fer a cup o' tay. That Oi would."

"So what do you do?"

"We go t' the pubs. If yer skint yer kin 'ang around outside and 'ope someone buys yer a meal if yer lets 'im 'ave a quick one. If yer got an 'usband or a reg'lar 'e'll bring sommat. Like Bobby. 'E brung me a poie." She gestured at the remains of the meal on the upturned box.

Lyla made up her mind. "Right. I've seen and heard all I need to. Eileen, I'll try to help you. Here. I hope you can get something warm." She dug in her pockets and gave her all the coins she had.

She went outside and sloshed her way back to Firefly, leaving the other woman looking in wonder down at the coins in her hand and then up at Lyla's receding back.

Chapter Twenty-One

When Lyla got back to Firefly, he looked at her reproachfully. She patted his nose and said "I'm sorry. But they're a lot worse off than you are. You've got a nice dry stable to go back to, and someone to feed you!"

She was wondering how she was going to remount without a block and was contemplating walking the horse to a place where there was something she could step up on, when a familiar figure rode up.

"There you are, me darlin'!" said Finn Gallagher. "Jeb said you'd taken off up the road. I thought you might be going to one of the pubs." He grinned.

Lyla thought she should object to this term of address but after a moment, realized she liked it. "Very amusing!" she replied, "Though as a matter of fact, I was just thinking I might need to go to one to find a block or something to help me up onto Firefly. You don't know how lucky you are, not having to ride side saddle!"

"But you couldn't ride that horse of yours any other way, Miss Worsley. He's much too big!"

Lyla blushed, realizing he must have the mental image of her with her legs straddled wide across Firefly's wide back.

Still smiling, Finn dismounted and came towards her. "Let me help you."

She was expecting him to make a cup with his hands that she could put her foot into, but instead, he put his hands around her waist and lifted her swiftly onto the saddle.

"Oh!" she said, blushing again and making a to-do of placing her leg over the pommel and arranging her skirts. "Thank you, Mr. Gallagher."

"Always at your service, Miss Worsley." He grinned up at her. "But you haven't told me what you're doing here. I know the living arrangement with Miss Potter must be somewhat confining, charming though she is, but I hardly think you need to set yourself up in one of these tents. Indeed, it might send altogether the wrong message. A message I would, however, most readily respond to. I would be your most persistent client."

"Mr. Gallagher, you are, as always, being totally ridiculous. Though you're right about it being a little confining in that one room, especially when it's constantly raining so you can't go for a walk and there are no horses to see to. No, I came to see how these poor women are coping. And I find that they are in a distressing state! They can't make fires, so they can't heat up water or cook. There's nowhere to dry their clothes. They don't even have a trench for the midden. I'm sure the place is infested with rats. It's shocking and dreadfully unhealthy! And do you know most of them are actually soldiers' wives?"

"It's always been that way. In war time, when everyone is living in tents, the army can't do without them. They act as nurses and forage for food for the men. The casualties of war would be far greater without them. But in peace time, the army discourages marriage amongst the enlisted men and doesn't supply housing. The women simply make camp outside the garrison. But they have no official recognition or help at all, in war or in peace."

"But it would take very little to make their lives easier! Straw to cover the mud, some sort of simple roofed structure to keep things out of the rain and build a fire. If it were put up against the garrison wall it would provide extra protection. When I look at the way our dormitory-turned-house and stables were built, it's obvious they had money and materials to burn. I'll wager there's all sorts of materials not being used inside those walls. I'm going to speak to the lady colonel!"

"The divil you are!" said Finn admiringly. "Hats off to you, Miss Worsley, but I doubt you'll get anywhere. The attitude has always been that the camp followers are to be discouraged. Idiotic, when you think about it. Better to let the men have their wives and sweethearts. They perform their duties more happily that way."

"And that's what I shall tell her. Thank you, Mr. Gallagher." Lyla nodded to him and clicked up Firefly, turning him back towards the garrison gate.

Watching her leave, Finn shook his head. "My God, what a woman," he muttered. "What a woman!"

Lyla rode boldly through the gates, ignoring the sentries posted there, just as they ignored her. Evidently a woman was not deemed worth stopping. She remembered the way to the colonel's house and trotted purposefully in that direction. But it had been dark when she was there before and she retained no clear idea of the size of the place. Now she went past the seemingly endless façade of the men's quarters, past the parade grounds where groups of soldiers were training, up a wide boulevard that led in the end to a group of individual homes, the largest and finest of which was that of the commanding officer.

She dismounted in the porte cochère and handed Firefly's reins to a uniformed lackey who came running forward.

"I have a meeting with the colonel's lady," she said grandly but untruthfully, "I shan't be long, but please rub Firefly down and give him water."

"Yes, ma'am," came the reply.

The front door was opened for her by a man in livery she took to be the butler. She sailed in, her head held high, ignoring the mud on her boots and the hem of her riding dress.

"I am Lyla Worsley," she announced. "I should like a few words with the colonel's lady."

"If you would be so kind as to wait," he intoned, "I shall see if she is available."

"Very well, but it is nearing time for luncheon and I cannot stay long," replied Lyla, seating herself on a padded bench by the door, but thus giving the impression she was doing them a favor by her presence at such a moment.

The butler bowed and moved off with that curious silent tread that is the hallmark of their profession. He was back a few minutes later.

"Mrs. Beaufort will see you in the conservatory," he announced. "Please follow me."

Chapter Twenty-Two

She was led across the black and white checkered stone floor of the hall into a large glassed-in area where fruit trees were already budding and spring flowers in huge tubs fragranced the warm air.

"But how delightful!" she said, holding out her hand to her hostess. "Both to see you and this lovely place!"

"Welcome, my dear Miss Worsley. Please sit down," said the colonel's lady, gesturing to a pair of basket chairs. "Yes, we are lucky, aren't we? When the garrison was built someone had the wonderful idea to alleviate the winters by putting in a heated conservatory. Warm water is piped in here from behind the fireplaces in the parlor. Thomas said you were in riding apparel, and suggested you might be more comfortable here than in there."

Lyla's immediate thought was that even the plants here had a better life than the women out in the camp, but she responded evenly, "Yes indeed. Please forgive me appearing like this before you, but this is not really a social call. The truth is, Mrs. Beaufort, I have come from the women's encampment outside the garrison wall. It's a sea of mud. That's why my boots and dress are in this state. But," she hurried on, as the lady appeared to want to interrupt, "nothing like the state those poor women are forced to live in."

"Forced? Who is forcing them, pray? It's my understanding they stay of their own free will. It's been the same at every posting we've been in. Heaven knows, we've tried to discourage it, but they always return."

"Of course they do! Most of them are wives of the enlisted men. Would you wish to live apart from your husband for years on end, and do you not try make his life as comfortable as you can?"

"I?" The lady appeared astonished that any comparison could be made between herself and the camp followers.

"Yes. It was obvious to everyone at the delightful ball I was so fortunate as to attend that you are responsible for everything that is beautiful and comfortable in your husband's life. He could not be happy without you by his side. Why, no one could have so quickly arranged this establishment as elegantly as you have: the flowers, no doubt chosen by you from this lovely conservatory, the perfect placement of the furniture and decorative items! And I'm sure you have often had to leave a place you have graced with your abilities and go to another! You, Mrs. Beaufort, provide the framework upon which your husband has built his successful career. Without you, he would not have been able to exploit the full range of his abilities or carry out his duties as well as he does. The camp followers have not your advantages of birth, resources and, if I may say, superlative taste, but they only wish to do the same."

Lyla wondered if she had gone a little too far with this fulsome praise, but the colonel's lady took it as her due. In fact, much of what Lyla said had the advantage of being perfectly true.

"It may be as you say, Miss Worsley," she conceded, "but a number of the women are... well, professional women. Are we to encourage our men to consort with them?"

"You know as well as I, Mrs. Beaufort, men will be men, whether we encourage them or not. And isn't it better to have them consort with what we know, rather than what we don't? I'm sure you agree that *your boys*, as you called them last time we spoke, should at least have, er... engagements, with women who are clean and live in sanitary conditions. I'm also convinced the frequency of visits to the public houses and the wrangles and brangles we so often see amongst the men would lessen if they had their loved ones nearby. You were kind enough to tell me last time we met how proud you were to have a special attachment to Her Majesty and thus to all women. Could that not extend to the wives and sweethearts of enlisted men?"

Mrs. Beaufort was an intelligent woman, more so than her husband, in fact. His preferment had been due almost entirely to his birth. Faced with these arguments, in spite of her initial distaste of the subject, she found herself agreeing with Lyla. She had hated being away from her husband in the early days of their marriage when no housing was provided even for junior officers. Since then, she had always tried to provide him with a comfortable home and wifely support. She was sensible enough to see that what Lyla said was right. Men would be men and there would always be camp followers.

Finally she said, "So what do you propose, Miss Worsley? Let it be something I may present to my husband! I hope I am able to be as persuasive as you!"

Lyla told her that she was not looking for a major financial outlay. With luck, everything they needed could be supplied from within the garrison: straw, of which they must have enormous quantities for all the horses, building materials for a shelter, men to dig a trench for the midden, and lime for the periodic dousing of it. Those simple things would make all the difference.

What Mrs. Beaufort said to her husband, Lyla would never know, but she was obviously successful, for over the next few months conditions in the camp changed for the better. Straw came in first, with new bundles delivered each week while the rain lasted.

Then the rain turned to ice and snow, the ground froze and the building of the shelter had to wait. However, by March the work began. As Lyla had envisaged, lumber had been left in piles around the garrison often covered with tarred canvas. It was this that had been stolen to make the tents, but enough remained intact to construct an open-sided shelter, hard against the garrison wall, as she had suggested. The roof was at first covered with the tarred canvas, but when the summer came, this was replaced with thatch. Once they were dry, the supporting timbers were coated with tar. It turned out to be a fine example of what the British Army can make out of nearly nothing when it puts its mind to it. The stinking midden pile was shoveled into a newly dug trench and covered with lime. While this job was naturally the least coveted, the men involved had fine sport shooting the rats as they emerged from the destruction of their home.

Lyla visited Eileen again. Eileen had told the other women about her and she was regarded as something of a saint. She deflected the praise, telling them their real savior was the colonel's lady. As a result, the women christened the place *Camp Amahlia* and as soon as the wild shamrock began to show its white head, they picked a huge bunch, which was delivered to Mrs. Beaufort with a note (written by Lyla):

> *To Mrs. Beaufort, the colonel's lady, with our heartfelt thanks.*
> *God bless you!*
> *The women of Camp Amahlia*

Whether the lady appreciated a camp with a very mixed company of women being named after her is not recorded. But she and her husband did visit it, once, in the early summer when the shelter was finished. The name stuck, however, and it was called

Camp Amahlia until, years after she was gone, it was finally dismantled.

When Mrs. Beaufort was an old lady, she read her long-retired and increasingly confused husband an article from *The Times* saying that, along with employing female cooks and nurses, the army was now to provide more housing for men with families.

"Well, my dear," she said, "you were ahead of them all. You thought the conditions of those women outside the garrison in Newbridge appalling and did what you could to improve them."

"Did I?" he replied.

"Yes, dear. We even visited it. You were much applauded. I remember it distinctly."

Chapter Twenty-Three

Lyla and Potter were sitting next to the hearth after lunch one day in late winter. Potter was mending the hem of one of Lyla's petticoats that had definitely seen better days, and Lyla was staring into the fire, thinking how much she wanted to get back to the horse fairs. They had not yet started up and she was both bored with the inaction and looking forward to working with Finn. She had seen nothing of him for several weeks and found herself re-living the experience of being carried in his arms through the rain and mud more than she would have liked to admit. The thought of his bending as if to kiss her made her shiver. Harry was still always in her thoughts, but he was somehow becoming more and more distant. He had never held her the way Finn had. He always treated her with the greatest of respect and had never even kissed her, even when declaring his everlasting love.

She had received a note from Finn a day or two before. He told her the first horse fair of the season was coming up at the end of March and he would be glad to accompany her there if she could be ready by six in the morning. Otherwise he would go alone and buy all the best horses himself. She had smiled at this and replied that of course she could be ready and if he thought he could out maneuver her, he was much mistaken.

The women were shaken out of their peace by the sound of someone bursting through the back door. In a moment Jeb was before them.

"Come quick, Miss Lyla. There's a wounded man i' th' stables and I don't know what t' do. The soldiers is after 'im."

Potter gave a little shriek and gripped the petticoat to her chest like some sort of shield.

"If the soldiers are after him he must be a criminal! Don't go to him, Miss Lyla! Jeb, tell the nasty brute to go away!"

"I can't do that, Miss Potter. "E's Nolan's brother an' 'e's in a dead faint."

Lyla got up immediately, grabbed her shawl and went in to the scullery to pull on her boots.

Jeb led her to the back of the stable and there, on a bed of straw, lay a boy of about 16, his ginger hair fiery against a stark white face. His eyes were closed. He could have been dead. Nolan was kneeling next to him.

"'Tis our Eamon," he said, looking up at Lyla. "Sure an' he come home this mornin' in a terrible state. Walked from Dublin with a ball in his shoulder. Told us he was at a meetin' last noight. Daniel O'Connor were talking about a free Ireland. Then a few lads got a bit o' drink in 'em and started yellin' in the streets — and the army got called out. A couple of eejits trew a few cobblestones and it were our Eamon got a ball in the shoulder. He took off and managed t' get home. Boot I couldn't leave him wi' me mam. If they ask about a young feller with the red hair loike he's got, they're bound t' get his name. So Oi brought 'im here. Oi'm sorry, Miss Lyla! Oi'm hopin' they won't look for him among the English." He looked back down at his brother. "He's dreadful bad, that he is."

Lyla thought swiftly. "We can't leave him here. If the soldiers come, they'll find him. Carry him inside, Nolan, and then ride and get Finn Gallagher. We've got to get the musket ball out. I'll do it if I have to, but I've a feeling Mr. Gallagher would do a better job. Jeb, you clean up and make sure there's no sign of blood around here. Nolan, your mother will have cleaned away all trace, won't she?"

"Aye, that she will. 'Tis not the first time someone's been in trouble, sure and it won't be the last."

Nolan picked up his brother. Lyla took off her shawl and covered as much of the boy as she could, especially his flaming red hair, then led him across the yard, praying that no one would see them. They went in through the scullery, across the parlor, and into their sleeping area. Lyla pulled back the bedcovers, then when Nolan laid him down, took off the unconscious boy's boots. His clothing was dirty and bloodstained, but she ignored it and drew the sheets up to his chin. Nolan gripped her hand wordlessly and left. In a few minutes he was galloping in the direction of the Gallagher estate.

Potter gave another shriek when she saw the limp form. "Is he dead?" she cried.

"No he's been shot by soldiers, but with any luck we'll be able to stop him dying either here or on the gallows," said Lyla. "He's only a boy, but that won't weigh with them."

"Miss Lyla! You can't keep a fugitive from justice in your bed! What would your dear mother say?"

"I think she'd say we have to help those who are the victims of injustice, and that's what I think too. Try to behave normally, Potter, dear."

"Normally?" wailed Potter. "Nothing is normal here! There's illegal liquor in the scullery, and if you're not consorting with fallen women, you're harboring criminals! Oh, how I wish we had never come!"

"Nonsense!" said Lyla. "If we hadn't come, you would never have worn that dress that makes you look so pretty. Wasn't it worth it?"

"No! Yes! Oh, I don't know!" Potter slumped in her chair, catching the tip of Sneak's tail as he fled from the cushion where he had taken up residence the minute she left. He yowled in protest and Potter vented her spleen by flapping her hands at him. "Stupid animal!" she cried. "You're as bad as the rest of them!"

Meanwhile, Lyla had gone back into the bedroom and placed her hand on the unconscious boy's forehead. He was very hot. She pulled back some of the covers and saw that his wound had started bleeding again.

"Potter!" she called, "Get the *poitìn* from the scullery and bring me that petticoat you were mending."

Mumbling in a low voice, Potter fetched the whisky and gave it and the petticoat to her mistress. Lyla put down the bottle on the table between the beds and took the thin cotton in her teeth. She ruthlessly ripped a wide strip from it. Potter gasped and began to protest, but Lyla simply thrust it at her, saying, "Tear off another strip. Quickly." Shaking her head, Potter nevertheless did as she was bid, while Lyla folded the first piece several times, soaked it with the alcohol and placed the pad firmly onto the bleeding wound. She saw it wasn't actually in his shoulder. Luckily, the ball had hit him an inch lower. She pressed hard; the boy groaned and his eyelids fluttered but then he lapsed into unconsciousness again. "Now lift him while I secure the pad." Potter looked as if she was going to refuse, but seeing Lyla's fixed expression, did as she was told. Lyla wrapped the second strip of cotton as tightly as she could over the boy's shoulder and around his arm, then tied it off.

As they lay the boy's head on the pillow, Lyla became aware of the sound of horses and shouting somewhere outside the house.

"Potter," she said urgently, gathering up the remnants of the petticoat, "if you love me, you'll do as I ask without question or hesitation. Take off your shoes and put your wrapper on over your clothes. Unpin your hair. Then lie down next to this young man with as much of yourself and the open wrapper as you can manage over him. Cover his face with your hair. If you hear me coming, make sure he is covered up. Look as if you're asleep. Don't fail me!" She closed the curtains.

Potter's face was a picture of outrage, but to do her credit, she did as she was told. She pulled off her slippers and put them neatly on the floor. In so doing, she saw the boy's muddy boots and kicked them under the bed. She took off her cap and shook her hair out of its pins. Then, from the hook where it hung, took the wrapper she used in the mornings and put it on. It was an old one of Lyla's that she refused to part with, though it had always been too large for her thin frame. Then she put her cap over the boy's red curls, tucking them up as best she could. Carefully, she lay down next to her bedfellow and rolled enough of her body onto him that she obscured his outline. She placed her arm across his upper body and arranged the wide wrapper so that it fell over him, then lay her head down on one arm with her hair over his face. Her nose was filled with the smell of unwashed boy and the unmistakable scent of blood. She could feel her heart beating in her thin chest and wondered how it was that she, Eunice Potter, brought up with the strictest rectitude by a stern father, should be lying on a bed with a young man who was not only a complete stranger but a criminal.

But she didn't have much time to wonder, for a loud knocking came at the front door and Lyla's cultured English voice came clearly to her ears.

"Good afternoon, gentlemen, what can I do for you? If you're looking for the gates to the garrison, they're about a quarter of a mile down the road."

There was a mutter of masculine voices, then Lyla's voice again.

"Eamon Murphy, you say? No, I don't know of anyone by that name. There's a Nolan Murphy who works for me in the stables. I don't know if he's any relation. Murphy is a common name in these parts. In any case, he's away at the moment doing some business with my colleague Finn Gallagher. You know him, perhaps?"

There was another mutter of deep voices and then, "I can't imagine why you should wish to come into my home. There's no one here but myself and my companion. But come in, if you must."

There was a stamping of boots and then a male voice asked, "You have just the one room, then?"

"Apart from the scullery, yes. It's through there."

"What's behind the curtain?"

"Our sleeping accommodations. Surely you don't wish to see those!"

There was a mutter and the sound of boots coming nearer.

Lyla's voice rang out. "Does your commanding officer know you are forcing your way into a lady's bedroom?"

"Our commanding officer wishes us to do our duty. I must ask you to stand aside, Ma'am."

"But my companion is sleeping in there!"

"Nevertheless..."

"Oh, very well. There you are."

Lyla drew back the curtain slightly and Potter could imagine what their view was like. Her back was to the soldiers and the area was unlit. They had just come in from the light, and were looking into a dark chamber enclosed by heavy curtains. Their eyes would take some time to adjust.

She gave a slight snore.

"My companion is... is, well, she has difficulty sleeping. She often takes a little drop of the local whisky to help with her insomnia."

"A little drop for insomnia is it?" came the incredulous voice of a different soldier. "It fairly stinks of the stuff in here."

"Keep your comments to yourself, Simpson," said the first voice. "Thank you, Ma'am. We need not disturb you further."

The curtain was pulled closed.

"Feel free to look in the scullery before you go," said Lyla. "And there are the stables, of course. My groom is over there. He will be glad to help you." She paused. "This Eamon Murphy, he's a dangerous and violent fellow, I presume?"

"Yes indeed, ma'am," came the answer. "A regular brute. We're certain we winged him, but we need to put our hands on him for the sake of public safety."

"It's heartening to know we can depend on you," said Lyla. "Thank you."

"Thank you, ma'am. Goodbye." There was a clicking of heels and the sound of the front door closing.

A few minutes later, Lyla slipped through the curtains.

"Miss Lyla," said Potter, unable to contain her outrage. "I hope I am as Christian as the next woman, but to be thought a dipsomaniac is beyond anything!"

But Lyla couldn't answer. She had her hands against her mouth and her shoulders were shaking with suppressed mirth.

"I...I'm sorry, Potter, my love," she gasped at last. "I know I shouldn't laugh, especially with that poor boy lying there, but I couldn't think how else to explain the b...bottle on the table and the strong s...smell of alcohol. Your snore gave me the idea. How often have I heard my father snore when he falls asleep after imbibing too heavily at dinner."

Potter got up off the bed and stalked through the draperies. "I'm glad I afford you such amusement, Miss Lyla," she said. "I'm only relieved my father isn't alive to see this day!"

"Well, I never knew him," replied Lyla, controlling her mirth, "but I know what *my* father would say. He would say you were a regular Trojan. Pluck to the backbone. And I think so too! That snore was a stroke of genius! Thank you, my dearest Potter! You are a true friend!"

Somewhat mollified, Potter returned to her position by the fire, chased away the cat and took up the ruined petticoat. "I suppose I'd better tear some more strips," she said. "I expect we'll be needing them."

Lyla ran over and gave her a hug. "A Trojan!" she said.

Chapter Twenty-Four

As the hours went on, the young man in the bed slipped in and out of consciousness, and even when conscious, seemed not to take in what was happening. He stared at Lyla with glazed eyes, then closed them again, muttering something incoherent. She tried to keep his fever down by bathing his forehead with cold water, and squeezing some onto his chapped lips. She wondered what was keeping Finn. Perhaps he preferred not to get involved. Perhaps he was away. Perhaps... perhaps.

It had already begun to get dark when she heard hooves on the stones in the yard. In a moment there were voices in the scullery and Finn Gallagher came in, followed by Nolan.

"Thank God you're here!" Lyla ran up to him and took his hand. "I was beginning to think I'd have to extract the ball myself."

Finn smiled down at her, then lifted the hand that had grasped his and kissed it. "I would've been happier if that welcome were for other reasons, but I'll take it!" he said softly.

He went into the bedroom and bent over the injured boy, speaking to him gently in a lilting language Lyla couldn't understand. It seemed to calm him.

Then he turned to the others and said briskly, "Nolan, get these clothes off your brother and wash him in hot water with soap from head to foot. If I know Brigid, the kettle's on the hearth in the scullery. Miss Potter, please find something for him to wear, and help me to put clean sheets on the bed. Then please scrub your hands with soap in the hottest water you can stand, clean the largest needle you have in boiling water, pull some thread through a beeswax candle — beeswax, mind! — and thread the needle. Put it next to me here wrapped in a clean napkin. Miss Lyla, please have Jeb hone the sharpest knife in the house, clean it in boiling water and likewise have it ready in a clean napkin. Then bring some Basilicum powder and a quantity of clean linen."

Some of these instructions were unusual, to say the least, but they were all delivered with such authority, no one questioned them. Wordlessly, they did as they were bid and soon the boy was lying on a clean sheet, a doubled towel beneath his wounded arm. Neither of the ladies possessed anything like a man's nightshirt, and Jeb, when asked, replied he slept in his clothes. They had thought of using a chemise, but the young man was too broad in the chest and shoulders. So they wrapped him in another clean sheet like a toga, with the wounded arm and shoulder bare.

"Nolan," said Finn, "be ready to hold the boy down, should he come out of his swoon. Ladies, stand away. There will be a lot of blood."

He took the bottle of whisky that still stood on the table, poured some over the wound and with the knife made a neat cut where the ball had entered. Blood immediately spurted out, and Nolan, his face suddenly as white as the sheet his brother was lying on, crumpled to the ground. Lyla ran quickly forward and took his place. Finn put the tip of the knife into the wound and carefully probed for the ball. A groan broke from Eamon's lips and he tried to lift his head. Lyla lay across him bodily, forcing him back.

There was a tense minute or two while Finn located the deeply embedded ball, brought it to the surface and removed it, then quickly pressed the pads of prepared linen onto the wound. By then, the boy had swooned again. Lyla was able to stand up next to Finn and press her fingers on the pad of linen in place of his. Bright blood bubbled up, but she kept pressing. On Finn's sign, she removed the pad to allow him to shake Basilicum powder into the wound, then took a fresh linen pad to mop the blood. She watched with interest while he used the needle and waxed thread to sew together the edges of the ugly gash. Finally, they covered the wound with more Basilicum and a fresh pad and bound it tightly, pulling a strip of Lyla's ruined petticoat over his arm and shoulder.

They both stood back, let out their breath and looked at each other, their hands covered in blood and their chests heaving. But they exchanged a smile. Nolan rose groggily from the floor, shaking his head like a bear. "Sure an' I don't know what happened," he said. "Tisn't loike me to lose me head over a bit o' blood."

"Not to worry, Miss Lyla stepped in," said Finn. "She did better than anyone."

"He's your brother, Nolan," said Lyla kindly. "It was bound to be very distressing." Then she turned to Finn, "But how did you know what to do? All of it?"

"It's experience with horses. I would see wounds being treated by fellows with dirty hands, using instruments that were never washed from one horse to another, and then watch the animals get worse and have to put them down. I experimented in my stables and found that I had much better results when things were clean. If it works for horses, it's bound to work for men."

While they were talking, Potter had cleared away the bloody cloths and put them in a bucket of cold water to soak. "A soak and a good scrub is all they need," she said, "it would be a pity to waste good linen like that, especially your mother's napkins."

"Just don't hang it out," said Finn. "If the Redcoats see odd pieces of linen they might put two and two together. It's been known to happen."

"So this type of thing is common?" asked Lyla? "Though now I think about it, when the previous brigade of soldiers were here, one of the wives told me her husband was in Ballinrobe, dealing with some trouble there."

"Yes. That was all to do with stopping people going to Mass."

"Mass?"

"The Catholic church service. It's not permitted."

"Whyever not? I never heard of such a thing!"

"We are part of the United Kingdom of Great Britain and Ireland and controlled by the Church of England."

"Of course! We've been going to the old familiar service at the church inside the garrison and it never occurred to me!"

"We are an occupied people, Miss Worsley. We live under the iron hand of our masters. Some of us, like myself, work to make it a velvet glove, but iron hand it is."

There was a groan from behind them and they turned to see Eamon with his eyes open, attempting to rise from the bed. Finn went rapidly to his side, speaking urgently in the melodic language Lyla wished she could understand. The boy subsided and lay back. Finn went into the scullery and brought back a jug of water and a spoon. He spooned a few mouthfuls of water between the boy's lips. His brother stood anxiously by his bed until the lad closed his eyes again.

"You go on home, Nolan," said Finn. "Tell your mother Eamon's out of danger for now. But he's lost a lot of blood and he won't be up and about any time soon. He's going to need nursing. You can't take him home for fear the soldiers decide to pay another visit. In any case he can't be moved. Tell her not to be coming by here —

she's no reason to be visiting Miss Lyla and someone's bound to notice. Tell her not to fret. We'll look after him."

Nolan did as he was bid, but not before wringing Lyla's hand and thanking her incoherently in a mixture of English and Gaelic.

Finn turned to Lyla. "I'm sorry you got embroiled in this, but now he's here, he's going to have to stay. As I said, he's too weak to move and once he regains consciousness he's going to be in a lot of pain. Have you any laudanum?"

Potter went into one of the drawers and took out a small vial. "We can give him a drop of this when he needs it," she said. "He can stay in my bed. I'll sleep in a chair until he's up and about."

"We'll take turns, Potter dear," said Lyla, giving her thin shoulders a hug. "We'll have a regular timetable! But first, let us have dinner. I can't believe it, but I'm hungry. I hope you'll stay and eat with us, Mr. Gallagher. I'm sure there'll be plenty."

Their dinner had been simmering gently in the hearth since the morning. Most days, unless she was planning on baking a pie, Brigid would get a stew going after breakfast, then leave to deal with her own family. She would return to put their dinner on the table in the late afternoon, clear up, and get ready for the morrow, when it would all begin again. She was a wonder, constantly working but unfailingly cheerful. Lyla, who had always had a friendly but distant relationship with the farmer's wives at home, now saw how essential a good housewife was to the well-being of a family. She admired her enormously.

One of Brigid's great talents was the ability to make a little go a long way. Her thick soups or stews were made with small amounts of whatever meat was available and larger amounts of vegetables, usually cabbage and carrots and always potatoes. About once a week they had a pie, most often rabbit or pigeon. In the spring,

Brigid's extended family would invest in a piglet which was fattened up with slops over the summer and slaughtered when the weather grew cold. In the autumn, the ladies had enjoyed roast pork with apples, but with so many mouths to feed, the fresh meat was soon gone and all that now remained was the last of the smoked bacon and sausage. This was used judiciously to flavor their soups and stews. Though their diet was not very varied, it was always good.

The woman in question arrived now and came in, shaking the rain off her shawl and hanging it near the fire to dry.

"It's raining again," she said unnecessarily and then, "Oh! Mr. Gallagher, sir! I'm glad t' see you, that I am. How's the boy?"

Lyla wasn't surprised that Brigid knew about Eamon, even though she hadn't been there when he arrived. Secrets were hard to keep in a place where everyone knew everyone else's business.

"We don't know yet. If we can keep the wound from going bad he'll be all right. He's a strong lad. A lot will depend on the nursing."

"Sure an' I'll stay with him," said Brigid instantly.

"No," Lyla was firm. We mustn't do anything out of the ordinary. Someone would notice. Potter and I will nurse him. Anyway, you have enough to do. I've asked Mr. Gallagher to stay to dinner, by the way. We should probably eat as soon as we can, if you please. Eamon may wake and Mr. Gallagher needs to be on his way."

They ate a companionable dinner in spite of all being alert both for Eamon's stirrings and for anyone who might be looking for him. Finn was astonished when Lyla told him how they'd fooled the Redcoats.

"Let me shake you by the hand, Miss Potter," he said, suiting the action to the word. "On behalf of all my countrymen I salute you for your courage. You will be remembered."

Potter blushed and said she hoped she wouldn't go down in history as a dipsomaniac.

"A fine woman like you? Never!" he said, with a grin, then continued, "The boy's stitches will have to come out in about ten days. In the meantime the best you can do is keep the wound clean and get him to drink as much water as possible. Don't be surprised if his fever goes up."

Then he smiled at their anxious faces. "I'd change places with him in a moment, that I would," he said. "A ball in the shoulder would be a small price to pay for spending my days in your bedroom."

Potter tutted and Lyla blushed.

"I'll come back as often as I can without arousing suspicion," he said, and left them.

Chapter Twenty-Five

The women sat by the fire for a while, discussing what they should do. Potter's generous nature had returned once she got used to the idea of nursing a fugitive, and she repeated her assertion that she would sit with the boy. She would take one of the dining chairs into the bedroom and stay there throughout the night. Miss Lyla would go to bed as usual. There was no reason for her to spend a wakeful night too.

"To be sure, it's improper for you to be in a bed right next to him. For tonight we need not worry, but tomorrow we will move the wardrobe into the center of the area to make a divider. You will sleep on the other side of it. No, Miss Lyla, my mind is made up!"

"But Potter, you cannot stay awake night and day watching over him! You will end up needing more nursing than he! For tonight we will do as you wish, but tomorrow morning you will sleep in my bed — on the other side of the wardrobe if you wish, but you will sleep. After that we will take turns. You know how many times I've stayed with a horse overnight! No arguments! My mind is made up too!"

So that's how they arranged it, though Potter insisted on taking the major part of the night watches.

The first couple of nights and days, Eamon was very fretful. He swung between a delirious wakefulness and laudanum-induced sleep from which he would start up, his eyes open but seeing only what was in his fevered brain. Both women urged water and broth on him. Sometimes he would take it, but at others, the liquid would dribble from his mouth. Using boiled linens, they changed his dressing every day. Lyla kept an anxious eye on the wound, fearing signs of infection, but while the ugly gash with its lattice of bloodied thread never seemed to get better, it did not get worse. The cats would venture in, and even jump up on the bed, but either the uncontrolled movements of the boy in pain, or the sense that something was wrong, made them leave again.

Then, just as they thought they were in the clear, the next night Potter woke Lyla with the words, "I think he's dying, Miss Lyla! He's ever so hot and now he's started shaking all over! I don't know what to do!"

Lyla threw her shawl around her shoulders and went to Eamon's bedside. As Potter had said, the boy was shaking in all his limbs. His skin was dry to the touch and burning hot.

"It's the fever," she said. "It's gone up suddenly. I've seen it happen with horses. We need to try to bring it down. Bring a bucket of water from the scullery and get the most voluminous nightgown we possess from the wardrobe. We need to wet it and put it on his body. It's what we do with the horses, at least, not with a nightgown, but you know what I mean!"

Potter ran to the scullery. She was back almost immediately with the water and then searched the wardrobe for the necessary item. Lyla had meanwhile undone the sheet toga Eamon was wrapped in, exposing a broad white chest with a few whisps of red hair. She pulled the wet linen from the bucket and quickly wrung it out.

"It mustn't be too dry, but we don't want to drench the bed either," she said, shaking out the garment — it was one of her nightdresses she now saw — and laying it over the boy's body. Patting it and moving it around, she said to Potter, "Find some of the napkins we've been using for bandages, wet them and wrap them around his wrists and legs. That will help."

The two women worked for nearly an hour, re-wetting the linen and re-applying it. The shaking gradually stopped. Then a few minutes later, the boy's head and body were drenched in sweat.

"The sweat after the fever," said Lyla, "I've seen that happen with horses too. We just have to dry him and keep him comfortable now." She used dry napkins to pat down the boy's body, and re-wrapped him in his toga. She pulled the covers up to his chin and turned and hugged her helper. "I think we've done it, Potter! I think we've done it!"

Potter burst into tears. "I thought he was going to die!" she sobbed. "Oh, Miss Lyla, why are we here? The quarrels these people have aren't our quarrels. I don't know this boy from Adam, and here I am terrified that he'll pass away while I'm watching him!"

Lyla put her arms around her, patting her back soothingly. "You're exhausted, poor Potter. And no wonder. You need a good sleep. Get into my bed — and have a small drink of that *poitìn*! His Majesty's Army believes you to be a dipsomaniac, you may as well live up to your reputation!"

Potter tearfully rejected both ideas, but Lyla insisted, fetching the *poitìn,* and making her take a sip and then lie down, fully clothed as she was, saying she could get up in a minute. But it wasn't long before she was asleep on the other side of the wardrobe. Lyla covered her gently with a blanket. Then she pulled her shawl closely around her shoulders and took the chair next to Eamon. She sat with a blanket over her knees, the painted shepherd and maidens lamp glowing softly. All was quiet, the breathing of both sleepers even and natural. She had the satisfaction of seeing a hint of color returning to Eamon's waxy cheeks. In a while, the flame in the lamp grew lower and lower, before going out entirely. But by then, her head on her chest, she, too, was sleeping. No dreams of Harry disturbed her slumber.

Morning light was coming through the high windows when Lyla was jerked awake by a voice calling hoarsely in the language she recognized but did not understand. Eamon was awake, his pale blue eyes wide with fear.

"Shh!" she said quietly, getting up slowly from the chair, her body stiff from the unaccustomed position she had slept in. "Don't be afraid. You are with friends. No harm will come to you with us. Here!" She poured him a mug of water and held it to his lips. He swallowed it thirstily.

"I am Miss Worsley," she told him. "Nolan brought you to my stables to hide you from the Redcoats. They came searching, but luckily, we were able to hide you." To spare Potter's blushes later, she didn't go into details. "Mr. Gallagher took the ball out of your shoulder and my companion and I have been nursing you. I'm so glad to see you awake!"

The boy made as if to get up, but sank back with a spasm of pain.

"No!" said Lyla. "Don't try to get up. You'll open the wound again. Mr. Gallagher will be by to take the stiches out. You were lucky. The ball went into the fleshy part of your arm, not the shoulder. Now, do you feel you can eat something?"

The boy nodded. Lyla went into the scullery, where Brigid had already been and gone. There were some *blaa* under a napkin on the table, and a large basin of soup left from their supper the night before. They usually made their lunch from left-overs. She looked around for a pan to warm some up. How she wished she had paid more attention to what Brigid did with such ease! She found a pan under the sink and poured the soup in, but then couldn't see how to suspend it above the fire. In the end, she pushed it into the smoldering peat and left it while she made tea.

She hadn't realized before how difficult even that was. She burned the palm of her hand trying to lift the kettle off the fire, and it was so heavy! The cats wound themselves around her ankles, making her movements even more difficult, and Scamp did his usual trick of catching the ends of her shawl, which was, in any case, falling off her shoulders. Between dealing unhandily with the kettle and pots and fighting to keep her shawl on her shoulders, it was some time before she had the tea made. By then, the soup was warm.

She carried it and the *blaa* into the bedroom, trying to ignore her smarting hand, meaning to go back for the tea. But when she tried to help Eamon to sit up and eat, every movement made him groan and her wince. Finally she said, "I'll hold the soup on your chest, if you can use your other hand to dip the *blaa* in and bring it to your mouth." She knelt next to the bed and he did as she suggested.

Eamon had consumed most of the soup when suddenly Potter surged from behind the wardrobe. She had slept in her habitual black gown and together with her thinness and her wild mane of hair which had come loose from her cap during the night, she had the look of a mad woman or witch. Eamon started so wildly that the heaving of his chest almost knocked the bowl of soup out of Lyla's hands and the terrified look came back into his eyes.

"Don't be afraid, it's only my companion, Miss Potter. She has been nursing you day and night and only last night finally got some sleep." Lyla turned brightly to her companion. "Potter, as you see, Eamon is feeling much better this morning. He has even managed to eat some soup. The tea is made in the scullery, though it may be cold by now. Would you see if it's drinkable and if so, bring in cups for us all?"

But Potter was looking at her in horror. Her mistress was in her nightgown, her hair falling down her back and her shawl hanging off with a cat tugging at the fringe, on her knees holding a bowl with both hands on a young man's naked chest. For with all the movement, the toga covering Eamon had become loose. Potter didn't know it, for her experience had never allowed her to see such things, but Lyla looked, in fact, like an illustration in a magazine intended only for the pleasure of gentlemen.

She spoke sharply. "I shall take over with that, Miss Lyla. You are... not dressed for... for company."

"Yes, certainly, but please see to the tea first! I'm dying for a cup, and I expect you and Eamon are too."

At that moment, a heavy tread was heard on the parlor floor, and Jeb poked his head around the curtain.

Ignoring her appearance, he said, "There you are, Miss Lyla! I've been waitin' to see you. Mr. Gallagher come by a while ago. 'E were deliverin' some 'orses to the garrison but 'e said 'e'd come here after." There was a sound of horse hooves on the stones outside. "That'll be 'im now, I spect."

Lyla burst into laughter. "It seems, Potter dear, that I'm destined to entertain not one but three gentlemen in my nightgown." Then she shook the cat off the ends of her shawl. "Stop it, Scamp! At least leave me my shawl to preserve my modesty!"

Chapter Twenty-Six

Once she recovered from her shock, Potter was equal to the occasion. She shooed Jeb out, telling him to ask Mr. Gallagher to wait outside a few minutes. She made Lyla get dressed in the scullery, having first locked the back door. She tidied the bed, pulled her hair into what Lyla noticed was her best cap, and then finally warmed up the tea.

Lyla thankfully drank half a cup before pulling on her boots and going in search of their visitor. Finn was in the stables, talking to Firefly in the melodious tongue he used for animals and the wounded. Her heart gave a leap.

"Mr. Gallagher!" she said as naturally as she could. Then she continued in a low voice, looking around to see if anyone could overhear. "Eamon has woken up! The fever broke last night and he slept well. He's even eating this morning!"

"Thank you! A cup of tea would be very welcome," replied Finn in a voice loud enough to be heard in the yard. "And if Brigid left any blaa, I'd be glad of one."

"You're in luck, Mr. Gallagher," said Lyla, in a similar tone. "She did, and Miss Potter and I were just thinking about lunch. Perhaps you'd join us."

Inside, Finn went straight to Eamon. The boy looked very much better. He had color in his face and though his eyes still had the dull look of someone in pain, he was fully conscious. Finn inspected his wound and nodded his head.

"Healing nicely," he said. "Thanks to the ladies' good nursing. You should be very grateful, my lad."

Then he turned to Lyla, gesturing to the wardrobe dividing the bedroom.

"He won't need overnight nursing any more, and I'm sure you'll be wanting your bedroom back, but I don't want to move him until I take the stiches out. Can you live like this a few more days?"

"Of course," said Lyla, and Potter nodded without dissent. She would agree with anything he said.

They went together back into the parlor, Potter brought in the remaining soup and *blaa* and they had lunch. Lyla was quiet during lunch, but Finn was in fine form. He regaled them with story after story, keeping Potter well entertained. Lyla knew her feelings towards him had changed but didn't understand it. Could she be in love with two men at once? Her heart wouldn't behave when she saw Finn, but when she thought about Harry, it filled with a pain she could hardly bear.

At last, Finn turned to her. "As you know, the first horse fair is on the 28th of the month. I'll be here to pick you up early. Will Seamus be coming?"

"Thank you, I'm looking forward to it. As for Seamus, I don't know. Jeb tells me he's spending most of his days in one or the other of the pubs. Do you think I should write and ask him what his plans are?"

"It would save time if you just told him what *your* plans are. Tell him you're coming with me, and if he wishes to be of the party, he should be on your doorstep at 6AM on the 28th. If he shows up, he comes. If he doesn't, he doesn't."

"But I hate to dismiss him. He's been a faithful agent and friend for many years."

"It's a kind heart you have, Miss Worsley," said Finn, "Why don't you write to your father and see if he can't pension the old feller off. Pay him a quarterly remittance. Better still, send it to Brigid's sister Moira. She'll keep house and manage it for him. If not, he'll spend it on the drink."

"I didn't even know Brigid had a sister! That's an excellent idea!"

Lyla was relieved. She couldn't turn the man off, but neither could she tolerate have him getting drunk at all the fairs. She wrote to her father and he agreed with her suggestion.

Seamus didn't show up on the 28th, so a few days later she went to see him and told him what she was going to do. He seemed relieved. "You're a good girl, that y'are," he said. "Sure an' with young Finn to help, you'll not be needing an old man like me. That suits me fine, so it does."

By then, Eamon's stiches were out and he was up and about, gaining in strength every day. He was by now sleeping on a pallet in the scullery, which he was as much relieved about as Potter. He had petitioned to be allowed to go home, but Lyla was afraid the soldiers might still be looking for him.

"If Oi'm a-stayin'," he said finally, "Oi'm goin' in the scullery. Oi'm not used to the caps and petticoats, that Oi'm not. It's loike sleeping with me granny."

Potter was scandalized and called him an ungrateful wretch, but Lyla just laughed. "That puts us in our place, Potter," she said. "You remember I worried it might look like a… a house of ill repute in here, but apparently not!"

That response outraged her helpmeet even more. "Miss Lyla! For shame!"

The situation was still fraught with peril, however. Over the next few weeks she caught snatches of conversations in the garrison and knew the soldiers were still searching for the violent criminal who attacked one of their number in Dublin. Then her heart fell to her boots when a knock came at the door one day, and without thinking she opened it to find a soldier outside.

Chapter Twenty-Seven

"With the compliments of the colonel's lady," said the soldier, giving her a note. As she turned to open it, she caught a flash of Eamon's flaming red hair in the darkness of the scullery. Uncombed and wild, it curled about his head like a bright halo.

Luckily, the waiting soldier did not appear to notice anything. Lyla turned to him quickly saying, "I won't answer this now. I've just remembered. I promised her the recipe for Brigid's... my housekeeper's dandelion wine. I don't have it by me now, so I'll write back later. Thank you." And she all but closed the door in his face.

Her heart thumping, she leaned against the door thinking hard. They had to get the boy out of town, as soon and as far away as possible. She strode into the scullery.

Eamon was amusing himself dangling a length of twine in front of the energetic Scamp. He had escaped Potter, who, when she found out he could neither read nor write, decided to teach him both. Once Brigid had finished in the mornings, she took over the scullery table and turned it into a schoolroom. "You can't just waste your time lying about," she said to the young man.

Now he was feeling better, Eamon begged to be given some other job, but he was a good-tempered fellow and, if not a scholar, was making some progress. But what was more surprising was that Jeb, who had received the rudiments of an education in the church school at home, had seen what Potter was doing and had asked to join in. According to her, he was making great strides. He could do sums, read the newspaper and write in a fair hand. Potter had more than once remarked what a bright lad he was.

But the unexpected visit of the soldier from the garrison had alarmed Lyla. "We must make plans to get you away from here," she said to Eamon now. "But we've got to change your appearance. Your hair is as visible as an enemy flag!" She thought for a moment. "Now, who do we know who'd have horse dye?"

Stealing and dying horses to change their appearance was not uncommon. It was one way the locals evened the score with their English landlords. While it was hard to conceal the color of a bay or a grey, the appearance of black horses with white markings could easily be altered by the judicious application of black dye. There had even been instances of landlords buying back their own horses in this way. Lyla was well aware of the trick and at the fairs kept a sharp eye out for it.

Then she thought, "I'll bet Seamus has some."

When she told Potter and Brigid her plan, they all agreed it was best not to ask Seamus directly, for fear he would let it slip when he was in his cups. But sure enough, when Brigid's sister went looking in the old man's stables, she found an old pot of dye. It had obviously been made from black walnut hulls; there were still crushed remnants of shell in the bottom of the pot.

Potter, not for nothing a skilled dresser, cut Eamon's thick curly hair, and using a stub of a paintbrush made, ironically enough, from a horse's tail, painted his head and eyebrows with the black mess. Luckily, he was young enough that his beard was barely growing in, so there was no need to color that. Potter had him dry his head by the fire and then doused it in the sink. He complained vociferously when the cold water hit his scalp. It turned out that except for when he swam in the river or accidentally got drenched in the rain, he had never wet his hair in his life.

The water ran black, then clear. But when it was dry again, his hair was not black. It was a sort of odd brownish-grey. Much to Eamon's disgust, Potter decided to dye it again. This time it came out very dark and he looked a completely different person. In fact Jeb, coming in through the back door, stared hard at him for a moment before realizing who he was.

The boy's arm was still weak, but the wound had healed. He could leave now, but to go where, and how? It was Finn who suggested the answer. They were coming back from the latest fair, where they had bought six fine animals.

"You'll be sending these horses off to England in a week or so," he said. "Why not send Eamon with them? He's good with them, like his brother. You can concoct some travel papers for him and if he keeps his head down and his mouth shut he should be all right."

"But will he want to go? Leave his family?"

"If it means keeping his head, he will. It's a lot better than the gallows. Anyway, I shouldn't wonder if the Queen's Bays get their marching orders in another eighteen months, and the next lot won't know anything about him. He'll be able to come back."

When this proposition was put to the boy, he nodded enthusiastically. By now he'd been six weeks with the ladies and it was enough. With his new appearance he'd been outside once or twice, not into town, but to the stables where, as Finn said, he was good with the horses. But he was restive and eager to get away.

Under Potter's firm tutelage he'd learned to write his name, but now she forced him to learn a new one: John Potter.

"That was my father's name," she said. "He was a hard man, but a good one. If you live like him, you won't go wrong."

Although she'd never admit it, she'd grown fond of the lad and was pleased to think he carried her name, even if it was a false one. The day before he was to leave, she made him agree to have his hair dyed once more, just to prevent any red roots from putting in an appearance. Jeb traded clothes with him: a pair of breeches, a cap and a coat made in England. Lyla gave him a few English coins and they watched him leave. They couldn't make a fuss, or even wave, not wanting to draw any attention to him. Potter turned away to hide the tears that came to her eyes. "God keep him safe," she whispered. "God keep him safe."

Chapter Twenty Eight

They were on thorns for the next few weeks until a long and chatty letter came from Lyla's father who was delighted with the latest shipment of horses and commented that the new stable lad John Potter was doing well.

> *If you can believe it, he claims some sort of distant relationship with Potter, your dresser, though what she'd be doing with an Irish lad like that in the family, heaven knows! Besides, he seems to have some kind of defect. His hair is two completely different colors. Most of it is black but where it comes from his head it grows quite red. You must have noticed it, daughter, though he keeps a cap on most of the time. I thought it might startle the horses, but they seem to take to him all right. Poor lad! Such a disfigurement!*

Lyla chuckled at her father's misunderstanding, but his next piece of news made her suck in her breath sharply.

> *I saw Harry Blankley last week for the first time since the winter planting. He was looking for a new hunter and was very taken with that chestnut you sent. His wife was with him, though she usually remains in town most of the time. She doesn't like the country, apparently. Nice enough looking girl, though very thin and pale. Still, they seemed happy. He was all solicitation because she had a cough or a touch of the grip or something, so they didn't stay long. He asked after you when she was off looking at the kittens — yes, Dinah has laid another litter in the stables. Why she does that, I'll never know. In everyone's way. Anyway, I told him you were happy as a grig. He*

asked to be remembered to you. All that worked out for the best, didn't it? Just like I said it would.

After that, the letter contained little more than a few instructions, but Lyla wouldn't have known if it had contained a state secret. The reference to Harry took her whole attention. She knew the hunter her father was talking about. She could just see Harry on it: tall and handsome with his back ramrod straight. He had a wonderful seat on a horse. He was happy, all solicitation for his wife. But he had asked to be remembered to her. She sighed. She had just begun, not to forget, but to think of Harry as a distant memory. This letter brought it all back: the long summer days spent together, his promise to come back to her, and then that dreadful disappointment. The pain of it began all over again.

Potter noticed her mood and asked if there was bad news from home.

"Oh, no!" answered Lyla with a feigned cheerfulness. "Father was delighted with the horses and Dinah had a litter of kittens in with the horses again. She's so silly! It's a wonder they don't get trodden on." Then she added with apparent nonchalance, "And Mr. Blankley visited with his new wife. She has a cold, poor thing."

Potter looked at her narrowly, for, of course everyone in the house knew what had happened between Lyla and Harry. But she said nothing.

Spring had given way to summer and the days for Lyla were busy, though her heart was full. She went to the horse fairs with Finn Gallagher and laughed at his silliness but the ache resuscitated by her father's letter did not heal. She thought ruefully it was a pity she couldn't have it sewn up, the way Eamon's wound had been.

Meanwhile Finn was in a quandry. The first time he met Lyla, it was her pretty face that had attracted him, but that was almost immediately replaced by admiration for her bold way of dealing with him. In fact, it had brought out the devil in him. He could easily have sold her that bay, but wanted to see what she would do if he didn't.

He'd soon found out. She hadn't resorted to tears or cajoling. She'd walked away with her head high and then shown him she could spot a bargain at the fairs as well as he, and get there early enough to do it. He was used to old Seamus coming later and later and being satisfied with his leavings, but this woman was another matter. She was real competition. When he'd asked if she wanted to work together it was as much for his benefit as for hers.

But over the months, his feelings had developed into something quite different. After avoiding the lures of marriageable women for nearly ten years, he found himself falling in love with one who threw out no lures at all. While she always seemed glad to see him, she had a shell he had never been able to break through. He'd come very near to trying to break through that shell the night of the Ball. But the mud, the rain, and the omnipresent Potter had made the moment inauspicious. Then the adventure with Eamon had confirmed she was the woman for him. He was determined to break through her carapace and ask her to marry him.

Chapter Twenty-Nine

With the better weather, Lyla decided to visit the camp followers tent village. Their numbers had swelled with the coming of spring and summer. The place looked better, and certainly smelled better. Soldiers were sitting outside the tents with women who were evidently their wives or girlfriends. Someone was playing a penny whistle. There was a quite a festive atmosphere. Eileen gave her a wave and beckoned her over. Over a cup of tea, which they drank sitting on the wooden boxes that were now outside the tent, Eileen told her she had a real sweetheart now, and he was looking after her. And the colonel and his lady had actually visited the camp. Imagine that!

Unfortunately that was the day Finn chose to ride into Newbridge to ask Lyla to take a walk with him. The weather was for once perfect: sunny with a slight breeze. Not a cloud in the sky. It seemed a good omen.

"I'm sorry sir," said Potter, stepping back from the door to let him in. "Miss Lyla's visiting *those women*, though I wish she would not. It isn't seemly for a girl like her to be hob-nobbing with the likes of them." She gave a disgusted sniff.

"Sure and her warm heart makes her take on the world's problems," said Finn. "I've noticed her looking a little down recently."

"Oh, that's nothing to do with those women! She just got a letter from home that upset her."

"Not bad news, I hope?"

"Oh, no, sir! Only... well, it's not my place to say, sir, but since you're such a good friend, I can tell you she had a sweetheart who let her down in a dreadful way. Married an heiress! She's never got over it, poor lamb. And never will, I'm afraid. That's why we came here. The letter from her father spoke of him and his wife, and it brought it all up again. Such a shame!"

"Ah!" said Finn, for once at a loss for words. So that was it. She was mourning the loss of a lover. Definitely not the moment for a declaration!

"Please give her my best wishes," he said. He bowed to Potter and was gone.

Chapter Thirty

"What did Mr. Gallagher want?" Lyla asked when she found out Finn had visited.

"Nothing in particular. He just popped in. I expect he had business at the garrison. He only stayed a few minutes. Such a gentleman! You'd have thought I was the Colonel's lady herself, the way he bowed to me! He sent you his best wishes."

Best wishes? What did that mean? Why hadn't he stayed till she came back? He must have known she wouldn't be long. Lyla sighed. Hearing Eileen talking about her beau had made her feel even more alone. She spent the rest of the afternoon quietly staring into the fire, wondering if this was how she was going to spend the rest of her life.

Then a couple of days later came a letter from her father with shocking news.

> *You won't believe my news, daughter. Blankley's young wife has died! I told you last time I wrote she looked thin and pale and had a cough. She went back to London and it developed into an inflammation of the lungs. They did all they could. She saw the finest doctors. They took her to Bath for the waters. When that availed nothing, Harry determined to take her to Switzerland. Apparently there's a lung specialist there. But it did no good. She dwindled away before their eyes, apparently, and they couldn't even bring her home to die.*
>
> *Blankley has come back. He has closed the house in London and says he will make his home here. He blames the foul air of the city for his wife's death, although from*

all we knew, she preferred it there. He has come to eat his mutton with me once or twice and on the last occasion asked after you. Very properly, of course. He wanted to know if you were ever coming home. I told him I'd given you a year, and that was almost up. Not that you haven't done a marvelous job there. But I wish you would come home, my dear. A man doesn't like to be alone in his old age. There's no need for you to stay away any longer. Surely that man Gallagher you've mentioned could take over the agent's job? Talk to him, won't you? We can make the same arrangements with him as we did with old Seamus. I should think he'd jump at it!

Lyla put the letter down with tears in her eyes. But whether they were tears of sadness or of joy, she didn't know. Was she crying because poor Harry had lost his wife, or because he had asked after her? And her father wanted her home. Suddenly, she had a longing to be there.

Chapter Thirty-One

While she couldn't think of anything but going home, Lyla said nothing to Potter or anyone else. Over the next few days she racked her brain for a way she could arrange things to keep the business going in Newbridge. She didn't like to ask Finn Gallagher. He had always been generous to her, but after all, they were essentially in competition.

Then it came to her. Jeb had said he wanted to stay in Ireland. She'd always considered him a boy; she didn't know exactly how old he was. But thinking about him now, she was amazed how he'd changed. He'd been a skinny youth only a year ago, and now he was a man. She knew Nolan's sister Maeve had been a frequent visitor to the stables and not only to get reports of Eamon. But as far as she knew, he hadn't been successful in finding a cottage to fix up. She'd asked about it once and he'd told her that it was as Seamus had said. There was nothing available that anyone would want. "No offense, Miss Lyla," he said, "But I ain't staying a stable lad all me days. An' I'd want me wife to 'ave summat nice. Not an old shack of a cottage."

Then, too, Jeb had become indispensable to her at the horse fairs. He knew what to look for as well as she. In fact, he had gone to the last one alone with Finn, because she had dropped the kettle on her foot and her toes were so bruised she knew she couldn't manage all the walking. He'd come back with some fine animals and Finn had nothing but good to say about him.

"He's a good lad," he had said. "He looks at you straight and the dealers trust him. He has a good eye for the horses. Sure and he lacks certain attractions you have, Miss Worsley, but we can't blame him for that."

The next day she went to the stables. Jeb was sweeping out the stalls. As he opened and closed their gates, the horses all nickered in recognition; he said their names and spoke softly to each one. They stood quietly while he did his job, obviously trusting him.

"Jeb," she said without preamble, "You remember you told me you wanted to stay in Ireland because you liked being in charge, and didn't want to be a stable boy all your life? Well, I have a proposal for you. I have to go back to England, but I'd like you to stay here and continue to work for me. I need you to go the fairs and buy horses for us like Mr. O'Donoghue used to. I will increase your wages, of course. I haven't spoken to Mr. Gallagher yet, but I'm sure he'd help you. But it all depends if I can get the lease for the property and stables extended. If I can, you can live here — I mean in our converted dormitory."

Jeb dropped the broom and stood, open mouthed. "Y'mean, live in there?" He gestured towards their house.

He seemed more overawed by that than by the offer of a big job promotion.

"Yes. I think your young lady would like it more than an old cottage, don't you?"

"Would she? She'd kiss the ground, I shouldn't wonder!"

"And kiss you too, I expect," teased Lyla.

Jeb blushed like a school boy.

Lyla smiled and patted him on the shoulder. "But don't say anything yet. I have to write to the land agent in Dublin. They may refuse."

But they didn't. The answer came more quickly than Lyla had imagined. She spoke to Seamus and explained that her father wanted her to come home and she was leaving Jeb in charge of buying the horses. But until he got the hang of it, she was depending on Seamus to help him with the paperwork, especially that of transporting the horses to England.

"Sure and we'll be sorry to lose you, darlin'," said Seamus, "but your Da's wishes come first, so they do. Jeb's a good lad. And from what Oi hear, he's got a red-haired reason fer stayin'."

"Yes, and I've obtained an extension on the lease of the whole property, the stables and dormitory-house so he, or they, can live there. If he's to be our...," she was going to say *agent*, but didn't want to hurt the old man's feelings, "*manager*, he needs to live somewhere a bit better than in the stables."

Seamus agreed to help. Potter was delighted. Jeb was walking around with such a smile on his face it looked as if it might crack. The only person she needed to tell was Finn Gallagher. Lyla found she didn't want to tell him she was leaving. He was what she would miss most. Although recently he had been rather distant. She didn't know why. In the end she took refuge in a half-lie.

"Mr. Gallagher," she said, the next time she saw him. "I must tell you Potter and I are returning to England at the end of the month. My father has said I must come home."

Finn's heart sank. Except for going to the fairs, he had deliberately avoided Lyla these last weeks, thinking she needed time to get over her renewed sorrow. He looked at her hard. "You'll be much missed," he said seriously. Then his blue eyes twinkled. "Sure and I won't get anything like the bargains I've been getting without you to dazzle the dealers."

"And I'll miss your Blarney, Mr. Gallagher," she said. "But Jeb is staying here and he'll be our... well, he'll do Seamus's job. I trust you to help him. You will, won't you?"

"I will, if you use the magic spell. You remember it?"

Lyla tried to make her voice light, but her throat was constricted as she said, "Finn, my dear, will you please help Jeb as much as you can?"

"To hear those words on your lips, Lyla," he said, using her name for the first time, "I'd help the divil himself."

As soon as he could, Finn asked Potter what had brought about the sudden departure.

"Her father did ask her to come back, that's true," she said. "But if you want my opinion, it was the news that Mrs. Blankley died that did it. She never talked about going home before that."

"And Mrs. Blankley was…?"

"Oh, the heiress her sweetheart married instead of her."

"I see," said Finn. And he did. It was too late. He'd missed his chance. She was going home and would no doubt marry the man she loved as soon as it was proper to do so.

Chapter Thirty-Two

Lyla and Finn hardly saw each other during the whirlwind of the ladies' departure. Finn deliberately stayed away, unable to bear to watch the preparations for her leaving. Lyla missed him and wondered why she saw so little of him but her heart was so full of the desire to go home to Harry she pushed those thoughts away.

She said her goodbyes to the ladies inside and outside the garrison and made arrangements for Jeb while Potter was only too pleased to stay indoors, carefully packing everything they'd brought with them back into the trunks and bandboxes. She shook her head over one missing petticoat and one ruined tablecloth.

"That boy!" she said. "You wait till I see him! To think we spoiled that linen for him!"

"Potter, you fraud!" exclaimed Lyla. "You couldn't do enough for Eamon. Admit it, you'll be glad to see him. According to my father he still goes by the name of John Potter and claims you for a distant relative!"

"Hrumpf!"

"Anyway, I'd like to leave that tablecloth for Jeb and his bride-to-be, and surely we can leave them a few settings of that china too."

"Your mother's china?" If Lyla had said she was proposing to leave Jeb her chemises, Potter could not have been more horrified.

"Yes, you were commenting yourself about how many place settings there were! I shall leave a set of six of everything as a wedding gift. We'll put the tablecloth on the table and set it with the china. Just think how surprised and happy they will be!"

Maeve's family was staunchly Catholic but no services other than those of the Church of England were permitted. Catholic wedding ceremonies were held in secret in the home, if at all. Lyla proposed the dormitory for the service and wedding breakfast. She felt that the authorities would hardly question the wedding of an Englishman in an English home. The underground priest agreed after much persuasion to marry the couple even though Jeb was not of the faith, so long as he promised to raise their children Catholic.

So a Catholic service was held in their home the morning of their departure, so that Lyla and Potter were able to attend before leaving for Dublin. They would spend the night in a hotel there, before sailing (God and the winds willing) to Newcastle the next day. It was all in Latin, which no one really understood. But it was clear when the time came for the groom to put the ring on his bride's finger. It was not the custom for her to put one on his.

Then there was joyous celebrating, which apparently could carry on for days. Though it was still only mid-morning, mead and *poitìn* flowed freely. Brigid, her sister Moira, and Maeve's mother had been cooking for days. For Moira, it was a rehearsal for her own wedding which was to be the following month. She was moving away to her husband's farm a few miles off, and Brigid was taking over as Seamus' housekeeper. This had been an enormous relief to Lyla. She hadn't wanted to turn Brigid off but knew they couldn't afford to keep her on while paying Seamus's pension and Jeb's increased wage. Seamus himself was the life and soul of the party and in the end had to be carried home by six strong men.

From the scullery arrived heaping platters: potatoes in all their guises from pancakes to colcannon, several meat pies and a large fruit cake liberally doused with whisky. Maeve couldn't understand why the mistress's china was still on the table. She had wept with joy and disbelief when told she was to inherit the house with all the furniture. She promised to polish it every day. Now she wept again at the glory of having china to put in the ornate French cupboard. However, her tears stopped quickly enough when Nolan grabbed a cup for a toast.

"You'll not be touchin' it, our Nolan," she cried. "A big lug like you usin' those fine things? Sure an that'll be the day!"

She snatched the cup from him and then carefully put it all away, avoiding Rascal, who was, as usual, on top of the cupboard, swatting at her veil. The cats were to stay with the newlyweds. This was their home.

Lyla was very disappointed when Finn didn't come to the wedding ceremony. He only showed up when she and Potter were making their farewells. He had a haunch of venison in a sack over his shoulder. Brigid and Moira fell on it with exclamations of thanks and carried it off to the fireplace for roasting. He kissed Potter soundly on the cheek, saying how much he would miss her. His goodbye to Lyla was much more subdued. He took her hand and looked as if he was going to say something more, but in the end merely bowed and wished her a safe journey. Then he handed her up into Seamus's old coach with its comfortless seats and glassless windows.

Anyone watching him as the vehicle lumbered off with Firefly tethered behind would have seen his jaw set and his eyes follow it till it was out of sight. Then he turned and walked slowly back to where his horse was tethered. He didn't have the heart to participate in a celebration of love.

Chapter Thirty-Three

The journey back to England was as exhausting as the one to Newbridge had been, and both ladies were relieved when the carriage rolled at last up the leafy driveway to the horse farm. Lyla's father was gratifyingly pleased to see her. He hadn't realized how much work she did with the horses until she wasn't there to do it. They'd lost a foal in an awkward birthing, and he heard the grooms muttering that if Miss Lyla had been there things would have been different.

"Now we can be comfortable again!" he said. "We need you here, daughter."

But if Mr. Worsley found things more comfortable, the same could not be said of Lyla. Her relief at being home was undercut by disappointment. She had somehow expected Harry to be there to greet her, to take her in his arms, for them to walk the leafy lanes and sit beneath the spreading chestnuts as before. But of course, he was not. In fact, he didn't come the first day, or even the first week. It was not fatigue from the trip but a series of endless questions that kept her awake at night. When would she see Harry? Why had he not come? Didn't he love her anymore?

In fact, he did not come for two weeks, and then it was only at the invitation of her father.

"Saw young Blankley in the village today," he said casually. "He asked if you were recovered enough from your journey to receive visitors! I told him it would take more than a paltry trip from Ireland to tire you out! Anyway, I invited him to eat his mutton with us tomorrow night. Wrote to the Squire and his wife to invite them too. They probably want to see you. Numbers will be odd, of course, but it's all very informal, between old friends."

Lyla's heart flew into her mouth. At last! But why had he thought her too worn-out for visitors? How odd!

She was on thorns all the next day and when the evening came, sat with her father in a fever of trepidation until she heard the butler welcoming visitors in the hall. But it was only the Squire and his wife. They greeted her warmly, saying how much they had missed her. She was glad to see them, but replied mechanically, her mind on Harry.

Then at last, there he was. He came forward and took her hand, smiling and saying how glad he was to see her. She was shocked, not only by how much older he looked, but by a pang of, what was it? Disappointment? Something was missing, though she didn't know what it was. The feeling left as quickly as it came, but it left a dark trace in her heart.

The evening passed pleasantly, however. Lyla was encouraged to recount her Irish adventures, which she did, making it all sound great fun, leaving out the episodes of Eamon's escape from the Redcoats and the camp followers' tents. They were amazed at the idea of her living in a dormitory, and astonished at the description of her first horse fair when she hadn't known about the necessity of slapping hands.

"This Finn Gallagher is not a gentleman, I collect," remarked Harry. "No gentleman would steal a horse from a lady like that."

This was, of course, exactly what she herself had said to Finn on the occasion, but now she found herself defending him.

"Oh, he is! He was very helpful, in fact. He was just maintaining the local custom. It was my ignorance." She suddenly had a vision of Finn's smiling face and twinkling eyes. "But there's no denying he has the gift of the Blarney."

And then she had to explain what that was. Harry looked a little dissatisfied when she was done.

"Sounds a bit of a blaggard, if you ask me," he said.

Lyla opened her mouth to retort but shut it again. Harry, with his typical English reserve, would never understand someone like Finn. She had a sudden vision of him making her laugh as he tried with his best blarney to persuade her that a horse they both wanted should really be his, or pointing out non-existent faults in an animal she wanted. No, Harry could never understand that.

Chapter Thirty-Four

As she lay in bed that night, she found herself comparing the two men for the first time. Harry was far better looking, of course, but there was no denying he had become a little, well... stodgy. Though perhaps he had always been that way. It was true he used to try to talk her out of things. Now he seemed so... worn down. That wasn't surprising, she told herself, with everything he'd been through.

Then the image of Finn's laughing face came to her. His life couldn't have been exactly easy. He was a younger son, so he'd had to make his own way in the world and learn how to do business with what was, after all, an enemy. Under his good humor lay a serious sense of where his priorities lay. He hadn't once suggested they should turn Eamon over to the authorities, even though if his involvement had become known he would have been in trouble and his livelihood would have been lost. He would have been *persona non grata* in the garrison. She wondered now what Harry's reaction would have been in the same situation. She was still pondering this when she fell asleep.

Once they were settled back home, Lyla wondered whether Potter might be let down with her return to duties as a simple dresser. But when Lyla asked her if she was happy, she was surprised by the answer. Potter told her it was a relief to be home, to know what her place was and to dine in the kitchen with her cronies.

"You know I'd follow you anywhere, Miss Lyla," she said, "but being in Ireland wasn't what I was bred to. It's hard when you've been used to being one thing, to be changed into something else. Over there I didn't know who I was, if I can put it that way.

Newbridge was so different. I have some wonderful memories and I'll never forget it. But yes, I'm very happy to be home. I know who I am here."

Eamon was working in the stables when Lyla saw him for the first time after their return. Apparently, he'd already been in to see Miss Potter, hailing her as his distant, and favorite, great-aunt. His arm had completely healed and he was full of energy. But what was most remarkable about him was his two-colored hair, black as coal on the bottom and bright red on top. He greeted Lyla as his savior and announced himself ready to do anything for her.

"You'd better ask your great-aunt twice removed, or whatever it is, to cut your hair," she said. "You would look more normal with it all one color."

"That's what Miss Potter said," he replied. "Sure an' I will, if you wish it, Miss Lyla, but everyone knows me as the lad with two-color hair. An' the colleens like it!"

"Well, it's up to you!" she laughed, "so long as it doesn't frighten the horses!"

She was back to spending most of her days in the stables, which was the one place she felt at home. There were horses to be exercised, looked after and shown to prospective buyers. Some of the horses she had sent over were still there, including a handsome black hunter called Mercury. He had a heavy price on him, which probably accounted for his not having been sold. He was a lovely animal, strong and calm, easy over jumps and with a steady gait, even over rough ground. He had been expensive, but worth it, and she was glad to see her father had not valued him too low. She smiled as she remembered Finn telling her if Mercury had been a bay, he wouldn't have let her have him.

"You mean a horse is worth more to you than my friendship?" She had asked with a pout.

He had looked at her seriously. "Now, darlin'," he had said, "You know nothing is worth more to me than that."

She thought about that now. What had he meant, exactly?

Lyla was there when Sir Laurence Breckenridge came by looking for a new hunter. The old baronet had died while she was away and Laurence had inherited the title, as well as the largest landholdings in the district. He was much taken with Mercury. Lyla had known him all her life as a bully and careless of his animals. She told him so and refused to sell him the horse.

"It's no business of yours how I treat my horses!" he protested, furious at being thwarted yet again by a woman who'd never shown him any respect.

"No," she replied, "but it is my business how you treat one of mine. Good day, Sir Laurence. I'm sorry to bring our discussion to an end, but I'm busy."

She walked away, thinking about how she was going to explain the loss of a good sale to her father, and didn't see his furious expression and narrowed eyes. She didn't care, anyway.

Chapter Thirty-Five

I know who I am here. Lyla frequently thought about Potter's words. Did she know who she was? She ought to. On the surface, things were back to what they had been. She now saw Harry nearly every day. He would ride over and come with her while she exercised one or other of the horses, but when they stopped to take in the view or admire a tree laden with burgeoning fruit, they rarely dismounted. The easy relationship between them had vanished. She felt a constraint she'd never felt before. Had he changed, or had she?

The day after Sir Laurence's visit to the stables, she told Harry about it.

"You know how awful he has always been to his animals," she said. "He was furious when I refused to sell him Mercury."

"Do you think that was wise, Lyla?" answered Harry, his face serious.

"Wise? What do you mean?" She was surprised at his response. "The man's a bully and always has been."

"Perhaps. But he is very important in the neighborhood. He's not a good enemy to make."

"Pooh! As if I care for his importance or if he considers me an enemy! I'm surprised at you, Harry! You were not used to be so lily-livered!"

"I hope you don't consider me so." His face was still serious. "I'm afraid experience has taught me to expect the worst, and I prefer not to tempt fate."

"How can it be tempting fate to refuse to sell a horse to Leaden Laurence!"

This was a name they'd laughingly given him years before when his heavy handed riding caused his horses to stumble more often than they jumped.

"It's true he's a poor rider, but the man isn't all bad."

"Well, he's not getting Mercury!" responded Lyla, and clicked up her horse.

But it wasn't too long after this discussion that she began to wonder if Harry had been right. Fate did indeed seem to be against her.

She was in a deep sleep she was awoken by a cry from her father.

"Wake up, daughter!" he cried. "The stables are on fire!"

She sat bolt upright to see him with a heavy cloak hastily thrown over his brocaded dressing-gown and pajamas, his nightcap askew on his head.

Fire! That most dreaded of catastrophes! Even if the fire didn't kill them, the horses would panic and could injure themselves so badly they had to be put down. Lyla leaped out of bed, pulled on her dressing-gown, threw her thickest cloak over the top and laced herself quickly into her boots.

She ran downstairs ahead of her father and straight to the open doors of the stables. In the darkness, she could smell rather than see the smoke. The bedlam of shouting men and terrified animals filled the air. Plunging horses were being led out — thank God there weren't many. Stock was low; they were expecting a shipment from Ireland in the next two weeks.

As the last horse was led out, Lyla called, "Is that all of them? All ten?"

"No, Miss," answered a voice. "Mercury's still in there. 'E was the one gave the alarm, with 'is bellowin' at the smoke. But we can't get at 'im. 'E's that wild! 'E'll kill anyone who gets near!"

Lyla didn't hesitate. She ripped a strip from the bottom of her nightgown and went to plunge it into the water butt that stood next to the stable doors. To her horror, it was nearly empty. Her boots squelched into the earth where the water was soaking away. She frantically pushed the strip of cotton into the bottom of the barrel and wrapped the wet cloth around her mouth and nose. Then, ignoring her watering eyes, she ran straight into the acrid smoke of the stables.

It was thickest right outside Mercury's stall. He was rearing up against the gate, over and over, squealing in terror. She ran to him in the smoke-filled dark, removing her cloak as she went and saying his name repeatedly in as calm a voice as she could muster. At last he recognized her, her voice, her smell, and stopped rearing. She threw her cloak over his head to blind him from what was terrifying him and tried to open the stall gate. But the iron of the latch was hot. Pulling up her nightclothes in a bunch, mindless of exposing her legs to the top of her thighs, she used them as a glove to lift the latch and open the gate.

Sparks flew up her legs from the smoking straw as she pulled the gate open, pushing against it. But she thought only of the frightened horse as she entered the stall, feeling for the lead rope she knew hung on the side. Still talking softly and reassuringly, she threw it around Mercury's neck. Saying his name softly over and over into his ear, she led him out. Behind them, small flames began to creep around the gate and lick upwards.

Once outside, she called, "Eamon! John! Eamon Murphy! John Potter!" The lad appeared out of the darkness.

"Take Mercury and find someone to tether him in the quiet. Leave my cloak on his head. He's terrified. It's still mostly smoke inside, but the fire is catching and there's no water. Someone must have pulled the bung from the butt. We have to rake out the burning straw before it catches any more of the wood. I don't understand why there's any straw there at all. It should have been swept out at the end of the day as usual. If we're quick, we can save the stables from going up entirely. Go! Hurry! And wrap something around your mouth and nose before coming inside."

"Sure an' I will, Miss Lyla," he said, "But do you put this on." He lay his coat over her shoulders before running off.

Lyla looked down. She no longer had her cloak and it was obvious she was in her nightclothes, now filthy and charred into holes in spots where the sparks had leaped up. She shrugged on Eamon's coat and ran back into the stables. She knew where the rakes hung and ignoring the stifling smoke and increasing heat, went back to where flames were licking up the gate of Mercury's stall. Without a thought, she took off Eamon's coat and beat it against the wood. Sparks flew up and burned her arms and hands, but she didn't stop until the flames were extinguished. By that time, Eamon and the other grooms had joined her in the stable and were spreading out the smoking straw. Then, at last, her father and the manservants from the house came forward with buckets of water, fetched from the pond at the bottom of the yard. They worked until the floor of the stable was a sodden mess underfoot.

Someone brought in a lantern and they were able to survey the damage. The fire had obviously been started on straw outside Mercury's stall. It must not have been completely dry, however, for it had produced thick smoke, frightening the horse and making him sound an alarm. When questioned, the younger grooms, whose duty it was to stay with the horses overnight, confessed they'd all been outside.

"We was enjoying a smoke and a jar," said Willie, a reliable lad of sixteen who had been with them for two years, "on account of it being me birthday and me Dad 'avin sent me a pipkin of ale. We dint know nothing until Mercury began to bellow. Then we could smell the smoke, and raised the alarm. But Mercury were that wild we couldn't get next or nigh 'im, so we set about gettin' the other 'orses out o' there. Then Miss Lyla showed up."

They all looked at her. She had used Eamon's coat to beat out the flames and stood there in her ruined white cotton nightclothes. She had braided her hair before she went to bed, but with all the activity it had partially unraveled and was falling in sweat-soaked strands across red-rimmed eyes and a face smudged with dirt. Her father was the first to speak.

"Someone fetch a covering for my daughter," he said. Then, with a horse blanket pulled around her, he led her gently to the house.

Chapter Thirty-Six

Harry Blankley came to see Lyla the next day, and found her lying on a sofa in the parlor, where she had reluctantly agreed to stay. The night before, Potter had carefully poured cool water over her burns and spread her special unguent on her legs, arms and hands. It was a recipe she'd had from her mother, a country woman. It was made of honey and cider vinegar with ground up marigold seeds.

Potter was horrified to find out she'd been up early and back to the stables that morning.

"You're to stay still, Miss Lyla," she said sternly, spreading more of the special remedy on her burns. "The blisters have to go down of their own account. If you burst them, you'll have scars. No arguments, for once, you'll do as I say!"

So when Harry arrived, Lyla greeted him and said, "Forgive me for not standing up. Potter says I'm to keep still for fear of bursting the burn blisters. But I recommend you sit six feet away from me. Potter's lotion is odd smelling, to say the least!" She smiled wanly up at him.

"You cannot think I care for that!" he replied, pulling a chair up close to her. "I came as soon as I heard. It's terrible news!"

"Yes, and the more I've thought about it, the more I'm convinced it was set deliberately, and the water butt emptied."

"I was talking of your burns, not the stables," said Harry, "There was no need for you to be injured! What made you rush into the thick of it? Foolish girl! There were men enough to do it! But as for it being deliberately set, it's the shock talking. You have been dreadfully frightened! Who would do such a wicked thing? No, mark my words, one of the young grooms was careless and let a spark fall on a pile of hay. I went over to the stables before coming here and they admit to having been drinking and smoking."

Lyla felt a surge of anger at the idea that Harry should consider her so weak as to be suffering from shock. And calling her foolish! She was sure Finn would have applauded her. She was even more annoyed that Harry should have taken it upon himself to interrogate her grooms.

But she knew he only had her interests in mind, and answered evenly, "Oh, I suffered no real damage, for all I look like an invalid, lying here." She held up her mittened hands and bandaged arms.

Harry took her hands in his. She flinched and he gently replaced them in her lap.

"It breaks my heart to see you in such pain," he said. "I hope those young grooms will be turned off. Without a character."

"Nonsense! If you had seen how hard they worked to get the horses out and then help with raking the straw and bringing water up from the pond, you wouldn't say such a thing. Besides, they've all been with us for years, except Eamon, John, that is."

"You mean the Irish lad with odd hair? Well. He would be my first suspect. It's well known the Irish hate the English."

"But he worked the hardest of the lot, besides giving me his coat because I'd used my cloak for Mercury! That reminds me, I need to get him a replacement. I burned holes in it beating out the flames. You don't have an old one you could let him have, do you?"

"No I do not and I wouldn't give it to him if I had!" Harry paused and then returned to his earlier theme. "I can't believe you were permitted to go into the fire! I would never have allowed it!"

Lyla was shocked at the vehemence of his reply about the coat, but was really incensed by his idea that she needed permission for anything regarding the stables.

"*Permitted*? Indeed, I needed no permission! Only my father has that privilege and it was he himself who woke me up. And surely you don't think I would have paid any more attention to you than I ever have!"

"I'm sorry you think that way. I grant your father has always treated you more as a son than a daughter. But you are a grown woman now, Lyla. I'm told you were parading around in your nightclothes. It's not seemly. I like to think if I'd been there I should have been able to persuade you to go inside and cover yourself."

Now she was even angrier. "I wasn't *parading* anywhere! I was putting out a fire that might have killed those poor animals! No one was thinking about my nightclothes or anything else to do with me! Our attention was all on the stables. And I hope that if you had been there yours would have been, too!"

"I'm sorry, Lyla, but I confess my attention would have been wholly on your safety."

"Thank you, Harry," she said, somewhat mollified by this answer. "But really, you must stop thinking of me as a helpless female. I'm not!"

He shook his head, but said no more and soon took his leave.

She lay there, thinking about this exchange. Finn would never have criticized her for thinking first of the horses! And if he'd been there he wouldn't have said a word about her nightgown. He'd have been too busy helping her. And he certainly would give Eamon one of his coats!

It was some time before she calmed down enough to consider Harry's response to her idea that the fire had been deliberately set. Was he right? Had it been one of the grooms, tapping out his pipe and accidentally setting a fire? But then she remembered the bung removed from the water butt and the damp straw. Whoever had come in must have been carrying the straw and had to put it down to remove the bung. You couldn't do it with one hand. That's how the straw had been dampened. The water had gushed out before he'd had time to pick it up.

She was still pondering when her father came in.

"Well, daughter," he said, "it's quite like old times. Blankley doesn't seem to be able to stay away. Nothing stopping you marrying him now, of course. He got a nice little pile from his wife so your lack of fortune is of no account."

Lyla was ashamed to think that when she received the news of the death of Harry's wife, that had been her own reaction. But now she felt stirrings of doubt. She didn't voice these, but said instead, "I don't know, father. I'm sure Harry is still grieving his wife. You told me yourself how fond he was of her."

"Pshaw! A man don't forget his first love, especially in circumstances like these. If he's willing, I don't see why you shouldn't be. I'd like to see you settled in the neighborhood. This place will be yours one day, you know."

He walked up and down for a moment, smoothing his thinning hair. "Talking of which," he said suddenly, "I hope you don't plan on turning down more good buyers, as I heard you did with Sir Laurence. It won't do to lose him, you know, for all he's a damn ham-fisted rider. He's of the first consequence in the area and it would be a bad business for us if he told all his cronies and they stopped coming."

"That's hardly likely. Even if he lied about why I wouldn't sell him Mercury, people would guess. Everyone knows what he's like. No, in my opinion, he'll keep quiet about it. But since you've brought it up, it's my belief it was he who set the fire yesterday. To get back at me."

"What?" Her father was aghast. "Are you mad? Sir Laurence creep around and try to burn down our stables? Nonsense! He's a gentleman! He might be angry and call you any name he can put his lips to, but that... no! Impossible! Anyway, whatever makes you think the fire was deliberately set? It's far more likely one of the lads was bosky and dropped the dottle from his pipe. No one's owning up to it, of course, but that'll be the truth of the matter. Sir Laurence? Never!"

"I don't mean he'd do it himself. He'd get one of his men to do it, of course. The lads swear no one went into the stable after work was done for the night. Why should they? They were enjoying themselves outside. And they're sure the straw was swept from the ground like it always is at the end of the day. And who pulled the bung from the water butt? No one could have done that by accident!"

But her father continued to claim vehemently that a gentleman like Sir Laurence would never do such a thing and that her burns were paining her too much for her to think straight. In the end, between his denials and Harry's, she was almost persuaded she was making it all up. But in her heart, she knew she was right.

Chapter Thirty-Seven

They were expecting a shipment of horses from Ireland, so Lyla was not surprised when, a few days later, she received a letter from Jeb. Except that it turned out that though Jeb had addressed the envelope, the bulk of the letter had been written by Finn Gallagher. The explanation was quickly forthcoming.

Dear Miss Worsley,

I am writing this on behalf of Jeb because he has been careless enough to get his right hand trodden upon and he cannot hold a pen. He hopes you won't consider him too foolish to be trusted with your business, and if I may add my voice to his, I can assure you that he has been a model manager in all respects. He has made excellent choices in his purchases and keeps the stables in prime condition. His wife spends her whole day polishing the French furniture in your erstwhile abode. Woe betide anyone who enters with dirty boots! Jeb appears to be totally under her thumb, as one might have been able to predict from that red hair of hers, but he's as happy as a grig. The only creatures who dare oppose her are Scamp and Rascal, who rule the roost as entirely as ever.

I am enclosing his reckoning for the purchases he has made and can confirm they are correct to the last farthing.

Seamus asks to be remembered to you and says to tell you that while Brigid's cooking is superior to her sister's, he wishes she were less keen on improving him. He says he only goes to the pub to escape her. But it's my belief she'll bring him around.

The Queen's Bays are due to leave us in November. I don't know yet who will replace them. I just hope it's not an entire infantry battalion! I'd have to take to selling boots!

Eileen sends you her best wishes and says she remembers you in her prayers. Not being of the faith, you may not be aware that the prayers of a fallen woman are especially pleasing to God, so it seems you are known in much higher places than most of us can aspire to.

For myself, I can only say that with your departure the light has gone out of Newbridge. Even Brigid's pies, which I now have to share with old Seamus instead of the lovely English ladies living in a converted barracks, are no longer inducement enough to take me there.

Please send my best wishes to Miss Potter.

I remain your most obedient servant, now and always.
O' Fionn Gallagher

Finn had been much on her mind and hearing his voice in the letter caused Lyla's heart to give a leap. The friends he sent news and good wishes from seemed so much nearer, and the closing *now and always* nearly brought tears to her eyes.

She sat down immediately and penned a reply, though because they had no mutual acquaintance in England, she could only tell him about Potter and her "relative" John, with the bi-colored hair. But talking about John brought her to the subject of his coat, sacrificed in the fire. That led her to pour out her misgivings about the fire being deliberately set. She said she hoped he would not think, like everyone else, that it was all her imagination. She sent her best wishes to Jeb and his wife, as well as to Brigid, Seamus, Eileen and all the people who had made her stay in Newbridge so memorable. She didn't know how to respond to the *now and always,* so simply ended, *your friend Lyla Worsley.*

Her heart was much lighter when this was done. Finn was the perfect confidant. He would believe her.

It was now full summer. It was the habit of the Worsley stables to leave the horses out overnight and bring them in during the heat of the day. The young grooms would stay out there too, pitching tents or sleeping under the stars. Lyla had begun to wake early, pull on her riding dress and boots and be outside when the horses were brought in from the pasture. The animals would be exercised while the mornings were still cool and returned to the pasture until the day began to heat up.

She was a little early one morning and arrived at the stables before the horses had been brought in to be saddled. She was surprised to see hay already in the feeding troughs. She couldn't imagine why anyone would have put it there. The horses wouldn't need it before exercising. They would have been cropping the grass all night. She walked into a stall for a better look and saw two dead rats lying close to the trough. Alarmed, she picked up a handful of the hay and could see tiny, slightly curved black-brown seeds scattered throughout. She recognized them immediately. She threw the hay to the ground, and ran outside in time to see the first of the horses being led in.

"Don't put them in the stalls!" she called urgently. "There are water hemlock seeds in the hay! Take them into the paddock while we clean it up!"

The grooms looked at each other in alarm. Water hemlock was literally the bane of livestock. It was highly poisonous and there was no antidote. Calling to each other, they turned around and took the horses back the way they'd come.

"We'll need pails of water and all the brooms!" Lyla called after them.

They spent the next two hours thoroughly cleaning the stables. When she was sure there wasn't a trace of hemlock left, she gathered the men together, from the head groom, who lived in his own cottage on the estate, to the lads who slept with the horses. She asked them about the hemlock. Was there anyone who didn't know what it was? Had anyone brought it in by mistake? Or for a joke? If they owned up now, there would be no trouble, but if they were found to have lied they would be dismissed without a character. They all shook their heads and looked serious.

"We wouldn't do that, Miss Lyla," said one of them. "You treats us right an' we treat you right. Wouldn't none o' us put 'emlock in the feed."

They all nodded assent and Lyla believed them.

Chapter Thirty-Eight

She dismissed the grooms and went slowly towards the house, thinking.

This had been no accident. It could only have been a deliberate act of sabotage. Everyone in the neighborhood knew their horses stayed out overnight and the lads stayed with them. There would have been ample opportunity to put contaminated hay in the feeding troughs. There hadn't been a lot, though, not enough to kill a big strong horse like Mercury. And any country person would have noticed it as soon as they looked at the hay, which they were bound to do.

Lyla concluded it had been a nasty trick designed to cause the maximum of inconvenience rather than real disaster. Like the fire. The hay had only been kindled outside one stall. Any serious attempt to burn down the stables would have been more widespread. Both seemed more like malicious mischief than real attempts to put them out of business. And who would want to cause them malicious mischief? They were on good terms with all their neighbors and customers... except Sir Laurence. She was more than ever convinced these "accidents" were his doing. He had been really angry when she'd refused to sell him Mercury. She could hear him muttering as she walked away. It had to be him! It was just the sort of mean-spirited trick he would play!

Lyla poured out her suspicions to Harry when he rode over to see how she was.

"I just *know* it was Laurence!" she exclaimed. "It would be just like him!"

"Sir Laurence?" he exclaimed. "You're being ridiculous, Lyla! Why should he want to do that? He's a man of standing in the neighborhood!"

"He may be, but he was a horrid boy, and people don't change. You remember how he'd tattle on us when we were children! That time he encouraged us to scrump the Squire's apples and then called the gardener down on us when we were in the trees! You know he did!"

"He only did that once! It was just for fun!"

"Fun, was it, to have to stand in front of the Squire and have a peal rung over us? And see him standing there saying he thought it was his duty to *inform* him of the *theft*? You may have thought so, but I certainly didn't. When he heard about it, my father wouldn't let me out of the house for a week, not even to the stables. I was made to *sew hems*! It was dreadful!"

Harry smiled. "And I got a beating, but I'd forgotten all about it till this moment. Really, Lyla, you're making a fuss about nothing! Laurence is perfectly pleasant now. Not the best rider in the world, it's true, but a gentleman."

"Well, I don't trust him. Since that event I never have and I never shall. He was livid when I wouldn't sell him Mercury, especially because I told him why. This is his way of getting back at me. I'm sure of it."

"I hope you're not going to confront him with your suspicions?" Harry looked worried. "I'd really rather you didn't. I'd hate for there to be bad blood between his family and ours... us, I mean."

Lyla ignored the implication of the last part of that remark and said, "I was hoping you would talk to him. Tell him we know it was him and threaten him with exposure if it continues. He'd listen to you more than me. He thinks I'm just a stupid woman."

"I? Confront him?" Harry was taken aback. "No, Lyla I can't... I mean, we're not even sure the events weren't accidents! It would be entirely improper of me to accuse him. No, it's out of the question."

He would say no more on the topic, and turned the conversation to her wounds, how they were healing, how soon it would be before she could ride again. Lyla was deeply disappointed. Harry had almost said *our family*, but how could they ever be family, if he wouldn't support her? If he truly loved her, surely he would. Unbidden, the image of Finn came into her mind. She knew *he* would support her, even if he thought her mistaken. But she *wasn't* mistaken. She *wasn't*.

Chapter Thirty-Nine

Later that day, she went looking for Eamon-John.

"You told me the girls liked you and your two-color hair," she said to him, when she found him. He was sitting with his back against the barn in the shade, whittling a whistle out of a piece of willow. He scrambled to his feet when he saw her.

"Sure an' they do, Miss Lyla," he said with a grin. "That and me Blarney!"

"I can well believe it," she laughed. "Would you do something for me?"

"I'd walk on coals for you, Miss Lyla, that I would!"

"Well, it's nothing as disagreeable as that. Do you know any of the maids over at Sir Laurence's, by any chance?"

"T' be sure an' I do — leastways, I've a mate over in the stables there and I've winked at one of the scullery maids a time or two. She dint look as if she'd say no."

"Oh, I don't want you to do anything that would lead you into having to make a permanent commitment."

"Whisht! Don't you worry, Miss. I'm not after making any promises!"

"Good. In fact, your friend in the stables might serve us better than the housemaid. I want you to find out if anyone over there knows anything about the fire and the water hemlock."

He looked at her in surprise. "Are you tinkin' one 'o them might have done it?"

"Not without someone telling them to. But keep it under your hat, Eamon. Don't give any hint we might have suspicions! None of your Blarney!"

"Righto, Miss Lyla. You can count on me!"

Well, she thought. *I can count on the stable boy, but not on my would-be husband.*

"I know I can," she said.

Walking thoughtfully back to the house, Lyla decided she would do a little investigation, too. She sent a note over to Lady Breckenridge, Sir Laurence's mother, asking if she might visit her. That lady had been suffering from severe arthritis for years and kept to her own apartments. Lyla knew she loved having visitors and this assuaged her guilt at visiting an invalid with the specific intention of confirming her son's involvement in malicious damage.

Lady Breckenridge hadn't seen Lyla for some time and remembered her as a romp of a girl. She was therefore surprised to see a well-dressed and even beautiful young woman coming towards her. She held out her hand and greeted her warmly.

"I haven't seen you in an age," she said. "How handsome you've become, my dear!" Lyla had put on one of the afternoon gowns her aunt had bought for her London season. It was in a pretty apple green muslin trimmed with broderie anglaise and had a very becoming matching bonnet. "What is the matter with the men in the neighborhood that you are still single?"

Lyla laughed, taking her ladyship's proffered hand. "There are girls just as pretty as I and with larger fortunes! Besides, you know, I have been away."

"Yes, I heard you had gone to Ireland. A wild, lawless place, I understand. I'm surprised your father allowed you to go!"

"It wasn't wild or lawless, quite the reverse! The local people were kindness itself. The worst were the English soldiers, and even they were quite tame!"

"Tell me all about it!"

For a half hour, Lyla regaled her hostess with stories from Ireland. The hand-slapping, the illegal *poitìn*, the garrison, her odd living arrangements, the food, the people she had met. She did not tell her about the camp followers or the manhunt for Eamon Murphy turned John Potter, and for reasons that she could not quite enunciate to herself, nor did she tell her about her friendship with Finn Gallagher.

Then she moved the discussion from Ireland to the odd happenings at the stables. She had told her hostess about the fire and taken off her gloves to show the marks she still had on her hands, when a heavy footstep was heard outside her apartments.

"I say, Mama, is there any tea? I'm..." Sir Laurence broke off as he came in and saw Lyla. She looked calmly straight at him and the blood rushed to his cheeks.

"Don't stand there like a block, Laurence," said his mother. "Make your bow to Miss Worsley. You are old friends, are you not? She was just telling me about the dreadful fire! Look at her poor hands! Did you know about it? I wonder you said nothing to me!"

Sir Laurence shifted uneasily from one foot to the other. "Er, yes, I heard about it, of course, but I'd no idea it was... er, that Miss Worsley had been injured."

Lyla looked at him, but he refused to meet her eye. There was a silence.

She broke it. "And I was just going to tell her ladyship about the second cowardly attempt against us. Someone tried to poison the horses by putting water hemlock seeds in the hay troughs. Can you believe it?"

"No!" Lady Breckenridge might be a titled lady, but she was a countrywoman and the idea shocked her profoundly. "Are you sure it was deliberate?"

"Yes, quite sure. All of our lads are very familiar with the plant. There could be no mistake. In fact," she went on, determined to see Laurence's reaction. "I'm convinced both that and the fire were deliberate."

She heard Lady Breckenridge's exclamation of disbelief, but kept her eyes fixed on Laurence. He flushed again, and said, forcing the words from his throat, but still not looking at her. "Rubbish! Everyone knows it was a spark from one of the lads' pipes. And it was quickly dealt with. No harm done."

"Except to me," said Lyla quietly. "I shall carry the burn scars the rest of my life."

She was exaggerating a little. Potter's unguents had worked their magic and it seemed there would be little scarring.

"If I'd…," he began, roughly.

"Of course, dear!" interrupted his mother," if you'd known Miss Worsley had been injured, I'm sure you would have told me about it. We would have tried to help in any way we could."

But Lyla was very sure that wasn't what he had been going to say. Guilt was written plainly all over his face.

Laurence stayed a few more minutes, still shifting uneasily from foot to foot, before saying, "I came in hoping for tea. But I see there isn't any, so I'll be off."

"It will be here directly, dear." His mother looked at the ormolu clock on the mantelpiece. "It's just four now. Why don't you stay?"

"Er, no thanks, I'll... I'll get some downstairs. "Leave you ladies to your gossip." With a laugh that attempted humor and failed, he left them.

Her ladyship had to re-hash both events over at least once more, still convinced they'd both been the result of accidents. Lyla didn't try to change her mind. She was certain now that Laurence had set both in motion. She answered her hostess mechanically and soon after tea, took her leave.

Chapter Forty

The next day when Harry came by to see her, Lyla hardly waited for the butler to be out of the room before saying excitedly, "I knew it! It *was* Laurence who set the fire and contaminated the feed. At least, I don't believe he actually did it himself, he's too much of a coward, but I'm certain he gave the order. I had tea with his mother and we were talking about it when he came in. You should have seen his face! Guilt was written all over it! He was red as beetroot!"

"Lyla, Lyla," cried Harry, clasping her hands, then letting them go as she winced. "You must give up this ridiculous nonsense, really, you must! He was probably embarrassed at seeing you after what you said about his riding. He knows it's true, but doesn't like to hear it."

"Oh, Harry, why won't you believe me? You loved me once, but now you won't even listen to what I say!"

"I *do* love you, Lyla!" He made as if to take her hands again, but thought better of it. "And that's why I cannot allow myself to be persuaded by this figment of your imagination. You've always been headstrong and liable to fly off at any passing fancy. As a boy I followed you, but as your husband, it will be my duty to protect you from yourself, to prevent you from getting into scrapes."

"Your duty to protect me from myself?" Lyla was furious. "I don't *need* a husband to protect me from myself! I need one who would listen to me, believe me, help me, yes, but not because he thought I was incapable! I need a husband who would support me. One who would love me for being headstrong and liable to fly off at a passing fancy. One who would love me for what I am, not for his illusion of me."

She fell silent, her breast heaving. Once or twice Harry made as if to speak, but seeing her set expression, gave up.

Then, once she had gained control of herself, Lyla said quietly, "You know, Harry, I've lived this last year in a fantasy, and I think you have, too. You imagined you had sacrificed your real love to save your family. But in fact you married a good woman who loved you. And even if you did not at first, I believe you came to love her in return. You thought you loved me, but really, you loved your *idea* of me. I thought you perfect, when the truth is, you are not the husband for me. You are a good, kind person but not... not *bold* enough. We should be at constant loggerheads. I would always be pushing you in directions you didn't want to go. This year of separation is the best thing that could have happened to us. I think it's made us see each other as we really are."

Harry started to respond, but Lyla stopped him. "No, let's not discuss it any more now. When you think it over, you'll know I'm right. Stay away for a while. You need time to grieve the woman you truly loved. She deserves that much. Forget about me as a wife and when you can think of me as a friend, come back. I'd like that."

She held out her gloved hand, and, after a moment, he kissed her fingers.

"I will," he said. "Thank you, Lyla."

Lyla went slowly upstairs to her room, where she sat, trying to hold back her tears. But they would come, and she wept. She didn't weep for losing Harry. She wept for herself. She wept for the end of the idyll that had been part of her life for years. She wept for how wrong she had been, how foolish. "Oh, Finn!" she said softly, "Oh, Finn!"

Chapter Forty-One

Lyla's conviction about Sir Laurence was soon reinforced by a report from Eamon-John. He came back from a visit to the neighbor's stables wearing the coat she'd given him to replace the one she'd burned. It was an old one of her father's and fitted him remarkably well.

"I treated me pal over there in t' stables to a jar," he told her. "Said I'd been after earning a bit extra doin' special jobs for you and t' Master, like special fetching n' carrying, y'know. Told 'im you was good to us lads, which sure an' none knows better than me, Miss Lyla! I asked him if it was t' same over there. He said nay, as a rule, it weren't. Sir Laurence never even notices 'em except t' give his orders. But just at the minute there was one o' the lads grinnin' all over his face saying he'd had a coupla special jobs for the Master and earned a tanner. I said as it must 'ave been a good job for a tanner, but seemingly th' other lad weren't saying what it were. I reckon it were the fire an' the water hemlock."

"I've no doubt you're right." Lyla thought for a moment. "A tanner is sixpence, isn't it?"

"That's right, Miss."

"Well, you shall have a tanner to pay for the beer and the information."

"The beer weren't but a ha'penny, Miss, and the information were free!"

"Nonetheless, you shall have it. But don't go grinning all over the place!"

"As if I would! But they tell me the fair's comin' next week an' I'll ask that colleen I told you about t'come w'me, so I will. Thank you, Miss."

He loped off, whistling like a blackbird. It reminded Lyla of Ireland.

She wondered if there was anything to be gained by confronting Laurence. She was sure he knew her suspicions and had just about convinced herself that it would prevent him from making any further attacks, when a couple of days later, she was astonished to see the man in question riding up to the house. She was on her way to help turn out the horses for the night. The heat of the day was over, the sun beginning its descent behind the trees. As usual, Laurence was slumped on his horse with the worst seat in the county, but he touched his whip to his tall hat in greeting before dismounting in the yard and throwing the reins to a groom. Then he walked back to her, smiling ingratiatingly.

"'Evening, Lyla. Just popped by to see how you were goin' along. Sorry to hear you were injured, and all that."

"You should have thought of that before you sent someone to set fire to our stables." Lyla was in no mood to be conciliating.

"Who says I did any such thing?" he swiped at the stone-covered driveway with his crop.

"I do, and I know I'm right. You needn't try to deny it."

"All right, all right!" He shrugged. "It was a silly trick that got out of hand. If I'd known you would get involved in putting it out yourself, I never would have considered it."

"So you admit it? And the water hemlock?"

"Stupid thing to do, but I knew anyone could see the feed had been tampered with, so there was no real danger."

"But why, Laurence? Why did you do any of it?"

"I was sick of you giving me the back of your tongue!" he exploded. "Never a nice word to say to me! Always talking about what a bad rider I am. You and Blankley laughing at me. I wanted to teach you a lesson, that's all."

He was quiet for a moment as they walked towards the stables. Then he stopped in front of her, but still didn't lift his eyes to hers.

"Anyway, that's what I came to say. I hope we can go back to being friends and good neighbors. Dammit, Lyla, we played together as children!" He held out his hand.

Lyla knew he'd always been a bully, but he had been part of her happy childhood and it was true she and Harry had always laughed at him. He'd never really had any friends. She felt sorry for him and her father was right when he talked about how important he was in the neighborhood. So she took his hand and said, "Of course, let bygones be bygones."

He lifted his eyes then and, fleetingly, an odd expression came into them. Then he bowed, wished her good evening and walked away, calling for his horse.

Lyla watched him mount his horse, a showy thing that Lyla summed up immediately as a slug. Poor Laurence! He never could tell a good horse from a bad one, much less ride it!

Chapter Forty-Two

After this reconciliation, Lyla seemed to meet Laurence constantly: whenever she galloped one or other of the horses over the hill behind her home, went blackberrying in the bushes that grew abundantly around the pastures, or walked in the woods that separated his estate from theirs. They talked of this and that: the new blacksmith who'd taken the place of old Davies in the village, the hope of every farmer in the county that the dry weather would hold until the hay-making was done, the prospects for the hunt in the autumn.

Harry had taken her advice and was keeping himself to himself, so she was happy to have someone to talk to, especially as Laurence never asked when the Worsley stables were getting a new infusion of horses. She never had to ruin their new cordial relations by telling him that in spite of their new friendship, she still would not sell him one. She went to tea with him and his mother, and Laurence came to dinner with them one evening. She wore one of her evening gowns. He looked at her with obvious appreciation and she was flattered. He must know many beautiful more women in London.

"My word, daughter!" said her delighted father afterwards, "You're a quick worker! Harry one minute and Sir Laurence the next! You'll be *Your Ladyship* before long, mark my words!"

"Don't be silly, father. You know I could never marry a man with so poor a seat. I wouldn't be able to stand it!"

"Tush, tush! What's a poor seat on a horse compared with a title and all that goes with it?"

But Lyla just smiled and said, "Don't count your chickens, Papa!"

The truth was, having got over what she now saw as her infatuation with Harry, she found herself thinking more and more about Finn Gallagher. She realized he was the perfect man. He was a gentleman, he made her laugh, he had a wonderful seat on a horse and he treated her as an equal. Why hadn't she seen that before? Of course, he was always complimenting her, but that was just his blarney. It was true he called her *darlin'* all the time, but he probably said that to all the ladies. It was just his way of talking. He'd never given her any real hint that he regarded her as more than a friend. She wondered if she could persuade her father to let her go back to Ireland. But no, she'd burned her bridges. There was nowhere for her to stay. She couldn't turn Jeb and Maeve out! Oh, why was she such an idiot?

Then, one late afternoon, Laurence came galloping wildly up the drive in his curricle. Lyla was in the empty stables, the horses having been turned out and the grooms with them. The new arrivals from Ireland were expected that day and she was checking the stalls prepared for them. They should have been there by now and she was wondering what had kept them.

"Lyla!" he cried, as she came outside, wondering who it was making such a clatter over the flagstones. "Thank God you're here! We need you! One of the young hunters is feverish and his nose is running like a river. We think it might be the strangles but you'll know for sure."

"Oh Lord! That can go like wildfire through the whole stable! Have you isolated the animal and thoroughly cleaned its stall? Burned its fodder?"

"Yes, yes, of course, but my idiot of a head groom isn't sure what he's looking at. Can you come and take a look? I came in the curricle in case you want to bring along your bag of tricks. I'm told you have quite an apothecary."

"I do, but probably the only thing I could use is iodine. It's good for cleaning around the nose and mouth, and you can put it in hot water for cleaning. And bleach, of course. I'm sure you've got both of those. What a pity the wild garlic is over. We give it to the horses for all sorts of problems in the spring and early summer. But I'll bring what I can."

She disappeared for a few moments and came back with a stout leather bag and gave it to Laurence, who put it on the seat in the curricle.

"Won't you come in for a moment? I'll just run for my shawl and bonnet."

"No, I'll walk the horses."

Pleased to hear that Laurence was thinking of his horses for once, Lyla replied, "Excellent! I won't be a moment."

She ran in though the back door and up the servants' stairs as she had done so many times before. The busy cook and scullery maid paid no particular attention, but when she rushed down the same way a few moments later, her bonnet on her head and her shawl around her shoulders, Potter was emerging from her parlor and raised her eyebrows at seeing her mistress dashing through the kitchen.

"I'm going with Sir Laurence," Lyla called, without stopping to explain.

By the time Potter arrived outside, Lyla and Laurence were already bowling swiftly down the driveway. They kept up a rapid pace until they arrived in the village, when Laurence drew the horses to a walk.

"Why are you slowing down?" Lyla was impatient to help the suffering animal.

"I'm saving the horses. I galloped them nearly all the way to you. I should think you'd be pleased. You always say I ill-treat my cattle."

Since this was indisputable, Lyla nodded and said no more. She contented herself with waving at people she knew, or inclining her head at the men who took off their caps and the women who bobbed a curtsey as the Lord of the Manor went by.

Once they were through the village, they turned into a path that she knew went around the Breckenridge estate. It was by no means the fastest way to the house. She asked where they were going.

"I told you we'd isolated the horse. He's in an outbuilding along here."

"That must be inconvenient! It must be almost a mile from the stables."

"It was thought best to keep the animal well away. Besides, it's not so far as the crow flies."

This was true, as Eamon-John, who had been to invite the maid to the forthcoming fair could testify. He had come across the fields on his way home and emerged through the hedgerow just in time to see the back of the curricle trotting up the path with its two very recognizable passengers.

"Now, where be they two a-goin'?" he wondered out loud.

But he knew he would already be in trouble for missing the afternoon turn-out, and didn't have time to follow. Whistling his blackbird song, he continued on his way home.

He reached the Worsley stable yard just as the cavalcade of new horses from Ireland arrived. They'd been delayed by one of the horses throwing a shoe. With them was a tweed-clad gentleman Eamon-John knew well.

Chapter Forty-Three

Lyla and Laurence trotted up the path for about ten minutes, then she was surprised when he drew the horse to a halt outside an abandoned cottage. The thatched roof was slipping over the eaves and the single window and front door giving onto what must at one time have been a front garden were sealed up with stout planks.

"You don't mean the poor horse is here?" she asked.

"Yes, on the other side. You'll see."

Puzzled, Lyla slipped down from the curricle, took her leather bag and stepped forward. The one-time garden was rank and overgrown. Weeds covered the path that led around the miserable dwelling. However, she walked boldly forward, not bothering to hold up the skirts of her well-worn riding dress when it caught against the brambles. When she got to the back of the house, she stopped, surprised to see neither stable nor barn where a horse could be sheltered.

Her surprise turned to a cry of shock when a pair of strong arms encircled hers, forcing her forward towards the back door of the cottage, where she was pinned while a large key was turned in the lock and she was thrust forward. Falling to her knees, she heard Laurence's laugh behind her.

"I said I'd bring you to your knees, my girl, and by God, I have!"

She scrambled to her feet and faced him, questions tumbling from her lips. "Laurence, what is the meaning of this? Why have you brought me here? Where is the ailing horse?"

"That's *Sir* Laurence to you! There is no horse, my dear. Just you and me. Look around. We are quite alone. Cozy, don't you think? I made sure there were candles, a bottle of wine…"

"What can you mean?" For the first time, Lyla felt a stirring of fear. "You surely don't mean to… to…"

"Well, let's see what the night brings, shall we? And after all, why not? People saw us driving happily off together and when neither of us comes home tonight, they will draw their own conclusions. You may as well be hanged for a sheep as for a lamb, as the saying goes."

"I thought you were my friend!"

"Yes. You were clever enough to work out who was responsible for the 'accidents' in your stables, but not quite clever enough to see through that! I fooled you royally, didn't I? You've spent your life making me look like an idiot, but who was the fool there? I? Your friend? Why should I want to be friends with a chit like you? You're a tasty enough piece, I grant you. Tasty enough for a night's work in a lonely cottage, but of no account after that."

He lurched to the rough deal table that stood in the center of the room and began to open a bottle of wine that stood there. An empty bottle was next to it, and Lyla realized he must have been drinking before he came to find her.

Her knees began to shake, but she took a firm hold of herself. *It's no good getting weepy and begging,* she said to herself, *he'd probably enjoy that. Try to appear normal. Keep him talking.*

She straightened her back and walked around the one room that constituted the living space of the cottage. There was a simple fireplace in one wall. Other than that, its whole contents were the table where the wine stood, flanked by two simple stools, and under the boarded up window, a rope bed with a stained ticking mattress.

"What is this place?" she asked.

"Shepherd's cottage," he answered. "But we got out of sheep a few years back. Too hard to keep or something. M'father told me but I didn't care much one way or the other. Never liked the country or anything to do with the estates, to tell you the truth. Too much riding. And, as you've told me more times than I care to remember, I don't have a good seat."

"You could learn."

"What, and have someone like you telling me to pull my shoulders back, sit up straight? I've heard it all since I was a boy. I didn't care then and I don't care now."

"But you do care. That's why we're here, isn't it? Because I wounded your pride?"

"And you went to my mother. My God! That gave me a start! I thought for a minute you'd let on it was me who set the fire and poisoned the hay! She don't need any more reason to be disappointed in me. Always telling me I'm not a patch on m'father."

"I had no intention of telling her my suspicions. I was hoping to see you. I knew I'd be able to tell from your face if you were guilty, and I did. You never were any good at keeping a secret, even when we were children."

"I fooled you over the friendship thing, though, didn't I?" He was slurring his words now.

"Yes. That was clever of you. But what makes you think I won't tell your mother the truth about all this?" She gestured around the room.

"Ha! I've got you there! Told her today you'd flung yourself at me. Said you were in love with me. That's why you came to visit the other week. Hoping to see me, making yourself interesting with some cock and bull story about fires and poison in the stable. But I wasn't attracted. You're too low-born for me. Told her I've got my eye on a woman in London with a title. Perked her up no end, I can tell you! So, if you tell her now I kidnapped you to this cottage, she won't believe you. Besides, everyone will say you came happily enough. Nodding and smiling all the way."

"Goodness!" said Lyla admiringly, though her heart was sinking. "You've thought it all out! I'm impressed!"

"Yes, not such a fool as you thought."

"I never thought you a fool, Laurence, Sir Laurence, I mean." Lyla lowered her eyes and looked the picture of humility.

He laughed and held out the bottle. "That's more like it! Here, have a drink. Do you good."

Lyla took the bottle and held it to closed lips. "Mmm," she said. "Nice wine. Let's sit down and talk. I'm so sorry not to have been here when your father died. He was a fine man. It must be hard for you, having to assume all his responsibilities."

"It's a damned nightmare, that's what it is. Meeting with the agent and the bailiff and lawyers. But at least I get to control the blunt at last. M'father kept me on a tight rein, y'know. Not that there's much to spend it on in this godforsaken hole."

"Then I imagine you'll be happy to get back to London. Do you enjoy the opera? Almacks? All the parties?"

"The opera?" He gave a bark of laughter. "You mistake your man if you think I like the opera! At least, not watching some soprano wailing on the high notes. I like the review, though, the girls and all that. Got to know a couple of nice little fillies in the chorus. One of 'em tried to put one over on me once, saying I'd given her a slip on the shoulder. M'father had to pay her off in the end. Hussy! Never saw her again. Pretty, though," he mused, taking another swig from the bottle.

"What about the parties, and Almack's?" Lyla was desperate to keep him talking. Her hope was he'd fall asleep and she'd be able to get away. The light showing through the gaps in the boards over the window when they arrived had faded, but the summer evening was lingering on.

"Parties? A dead bore, most of them. Bowing and scraping to the hostess, forced to make nice with a bunch of pie-faced virgins you hope never to meet again. And as for Almacks, they serve you nothing but stale cake and lemonade! Can't even get a decent drink, and all the tabbies watching to make sure you don't lay a finger on one of the girls! Ugh! No thank you!"

"Oh dear, it seems you don't enjoy anything in London! I wonder you want to go there."

"There's good times to be had, just not anywhere a girl like you would know! Got an excellent bunch of fellows who know where there's cockfights and dog fights, or a set-to between a couple of bruisers in the ring or out of it. And wenches not too proud to take a feller on. In the sluices, Tothill, y'know. That's what I want to get back to!"

"Oh." Lyla didn't know how to respond to that. She hadn't liked London and could even sympathize with his view of the parties and Almack's. But for her, it was because she truly loved the country and couldn't wait to get back to her horses.

Laurence sat there for a while, staring at nothing in the fading light. Suddenly, he put the by now empty wine bottle down on the table with a thud.

"Anyway, enough chitchat," he said, grabbing her arm. "Come over here with me."

Chapter Forty-Four

Laurence stood up and began to pull Lyla towards the rope bed with its unsavory mattress.

Her heart leapt into her throat, but as calmly as she could, she said, "There's no need to pull at me like that, Sir Laurence. After our conversation I know you better, and though I blush to say it, I'm by no means unwilling. Please just allow me to remove my bonnet."

He grunted, but let go of her arm. She took off her bonnet and placed it on one of the stools.

"Are there mice in that mattress, do you think?" she said when they were by the bed. "I know I'm just a silly woman, but I hate mice."

This was a complete fabrication, of course. In spite of the best efforts of generations of cats, mice infested the stables and she was as used to them as to the flies.

"We'll soon scare them off if there are," he said, flopping down on the stained ticking.

The bed creaked and sure enough, a mouse skittered across the floor. Lyla shrieked and ran back to the table.

"If you don't mind, I'm going to light some candles to keep those awful creatures away. Oh, look! There's some wood in the fireplace. I'll light a fire. That will make it much more cozy. It's getting chilly." She shivered dramatically.

"I'll soon warm you up, my girl," slurred Laurence from the bed. "Just you come over here."

Lyla giggled. "I will. Just a minute. I'll light a fire and take off my boots. We'll be much more comfortable."

"Hurry up!"

Lyla made a great to-do of lighting candles and sticking them in the mouths of the empty wine bottles. Then she carried one over to the fireplace. She piled up the logs, causing more mice to scatter. But these, she ignored. The wood was very dry, and by dint of holding the candle to it, she managed to get first smoke, then a small flame. She left the candle where it was and stood up.

"Look!" she said. "It's catching! Now I'll just take off my boots and loosen my stays. Won't be a minute."

Laurence mumbled something and Lyla sat at the table, making a great show of pulling at her bootlaces.

"Oh dear, they've got in a knot. What a nuisance. It's so dark! I can't see!"

She took the other candle from the table and put it on the floor next to her feet. She fiddled a while longer, actually untying and retying the laces, until she was rewarded by a snore from the bed. She sat still and waited until the snores became deep and regular, then, picking up the candle, she crept over to the man lying on his back with his mouth open. She had seen him put the key to the door in the pocket of his coat, but unfortunately it was the pocket on the other side from where she was standing. She bent over him and slipped a hand inside. But as she did so, wax from the candle fell onto one of Laurence's hands.

He bolted up, shouting, "What the hell? What are you doing? Oh, so that's your game, is it?"

She dropped the candle as he grasped her roughly around the waist and pulled her down, rolling on top of her. She shrieked, "No! Let me go, you brute! Let me go!"

The candle fell out of the bottle and extinguished itself immediately. The only light in the room was the faint glow from the fireplace. Lyla was crying for help and struggling vainly with her much heavier assailant when she heard the sharp crack of the cottage door splintering, flying open and crashing against the wall. A second later, the body on top of her was lifted off and sent sprawling to the floor. Dazed and breathless, she looked up into the face of Finn Gallagher.

"Top o' the evenin' to you, me darlin'," he said and smiled.

"Finn!" she cried, "Oh, Finn!" and threw her arms around his neck. A moment later, he was jerked back by her attacker. Laurence had scrambled to his feet and was attempting to throttle him. But Laurence was the worse for drink; Finn was stone-cold sober and furious. He kicked sharply backwards with his metal-tipped riding boots and had the satisfaction of feeling bone crack. Laurence howled, let go and fell to the floor. Finn was on him immediately, pulling him by the scruff of his neck towards the broken door.

What happened outside Lyla would never know, but sometime later she heard Finn's voice outside the window saying, "All right, you miserable poltroon. This is the story: you and Miss Worsley were on your way to your stables, but you upset the curricle in a ditch and hit your head. When you came to, Miss Worsley had disappeared, you assumed to go and find help. The horse appeared unhurt. You righted the curricle and looked for her but were unable to find her. The effort made you faint again and by the time you came round, the horses had carried you home. Repeat what I just said."

She heard Laurence's growling tone recount what Finn had said.

"Right. If I hear a story that differs by as much as a word, I'll be back for you, so I will, and this time the only way you'll be carried home is on a stretcher. By God, if you weren't too injured to fight back, I'd finish you off now!"

There was the sound of a crop against the flank of a horse, and the rattling of the curricle moving at speed. Then Finn was at the door, with a smile on his face.

"Sure an' I only have to take my eye off you for a minute," he said, "and you get yourself in a fix. That's the trouble when you live in sich a wild an' lawless place as Middlesex."

He picked up the bottle with its candle in the fireplace, and the one next to the bed, put them both on the table and kicked the smoldering logs apart. He turned to face her.

"Now," he said. "If you can remember the magic words, we'll get you away from here."

"Finn, my dear, please will you take me home," she said.

"By all means," he replied, "but first things first."

He put his arms around her and kissed her.

"Sure, an' I've been wanting to do that for many a month," he said, "Now, where's your bonnet?"

Chapter Forty-Five

When Finn arrived with the horses earlier that evening, he'd been very disappointed not to see Lyla, but soon got the message she'd gone off with Sir Laurence. The lads in the pasture with the horses had seen them ride by. This was confirmed by Potter, who was delighted to see Finn again and sorry Miss Lyla wasn't there to greet him. She said it must have been something important, otherwise she never would have gone off on the day she knew the new horses were due to arrive. And she had been in a rush when she left. Then Eamon-John arrived back in due course and added that he'd seen the curricle on the road that circled the Breckenridge estate.

Lyla's father welcomed Finn, saying he felt he already knew him from his daughter's descriptions of her dealings with him. He was delighted to find their visitor was a gentleman and had no hesitation in inviting him to dine and stay as long as he liked. When Lyla wasn't home for dinner, there was some alarm, but Mr. Worsley said in his usual sanguine fashion she was bound to turn up when she was good and ready. She was probably dining at Breckenridge House.

The only person really worried by Lyla's lateness was Eamon-John, her self-appointed guardian. He knew Lyla had been seeing a good deal of Sir Laurence recently, but he didn't trust him. He went into the house and charmed one of the maids into carrying up a message for Finn.

"It's been troublin' me, that it has," he said, after telling him about the investigations he'd done on Lyla's behalf. "That path I saw the two of them on isn't the quickest way to get to the house, not by a long chalk. 'Course, could be Sir Laurence is sweet on Miss

Lyla, an' wanted to go the long way round. He's been hangin' around a lot lately. But sure an' that's a puzzle, too. She knows it were him as set the fire and tried to poison the horses. As far as I know, she can't abide him."

Finn felt a stirring of alarm. He remembered what Lyla had told him in her letter and believed what the lad said. He went back into the house and asked Mr. Worsley if he could borrow a curricle and pair to take a turn around the neighborhood. Just for an hour. He was still feeling the effects of the long journey. He was told he was welcome to use anything he wanted. Having received detailed directions from Eamon-John, he set off and found his way without difficulty to the tumbledown cottage. A curricle was drawn up in front with a pair of chestnuts Finn instantly recognized as all show and no go, peaceably cropping the overgrown turf. As he drew to a halt, he could hear Lyla's screams. He leaped down, hastily tethered his horses and ran to the back door. This easily gave way to his boots.

When he had dispatched Laurence and they were ready to leave the cottage, he took Lyla's bonnet from her hands and punched it entirely out of shape. She protested it was her best riding bonnet, but he laughed and said, "We have to support that cad Laurence's story. You were tumbled out of the curricle. Your bonnet sustained irreparable damage. I'll buy you a new one as an engagement present."

"Whose engagement?"

"Yours."

"And who am I marrying?"

"That would be meself, darlin'. I'm takin' you on as a charity case. It's obvious I can't leave you alone here in these violent parts."

"Were you planning on actually asking me?"

"No. I'm thinkin' a woman who willingly goes off with a poltroon like Laurence, knowing he tried to burn you down and poison your horses, doesn't have the judgement to recognize a good deal when she hears it. You might say no."

"But a lady likes to be proposed to in the proper way."

"I'm surprised to find you so conventional, Miss Worsley, independent horse dealer, friend of disreputable women and shelterer of hardened criminals."

"Nonetheless."

Finn went down on one knee and took her hands. "This isn't the best time or place, to be sure, but Miss Lyla Worsley, dear heart, will you marry me?"

She pulled him to his feet. "It's the perfect time and place. You don't know how often I've thought about you these past weeks. When I felt Laurence being pulled off me and I looked up and saw your face, it was like a dream come true. So yes, Mr. Finn Gallagher, if you will take an unconventional woman like me, I will marry you, and with all my heart. Anyway, I need a new bonnet."

"You shall have the best bonnet London can provide," he said, taking her in his arms and kissing her so hard it took her breath away. "But for now, let's leave this god-forsaken place."

They went outside and he bent down to rub his hands in the soil and, grinning, smeared her cheeks with the dirt. Next, he reached up and snapped twigs off the gnarled tree above their heads. He pulled strands of her already untidy hair out of their pins and then stuck in twigs. "To make you look as if you've rolled through a hedge." He laughed and kissed her again. "You look like a delicious gypsy!"

It wasn't until they had both climbed in the curricle and were on their way home that Lyla said, "Your face appearing above me was so much like a miracle, I haven't even asked how you come to be here."

"When I received your letter saying you believed the fire had been deliberately set, I was worried about you," answered Finn. "I offered to come with the horses and Jeb was only too pleased. He was anxious about his first shipment."

"You're the only person who believed me. My father and H... my childhood friend thought I was being ridiculous."

"This is the man who jilted you for an heiress and who you were pining for while you were in Ireland?"

"How did you know about that?"

"When a woman repeatedly gazes into space and sighs and doesn't hear when you speak to her, you begin to have suspicions. And Miss Potter told me."

"Did she?" Lyla was surprised. "She's usually so close-mouthed. But you could charm anything out of anyone. Yes. His name's Harry Blankley and I thought I was in love with him." She looked up at Finn, hardly able to believe what she had said was true. "But I was in love with an idea of him, not the real him. I've been so stupid. I realized some time ago it's you I love. I've been trying to work out how to get back to Ireland."

By this time they had arrived at the village. Finn reined the horses into a trot. It was unusual enough for a vehicle to be passing at that time of night for people to look out of their windows with curiosity. When they did, they saw Miss Worsley, hatless and disheveled, being driven by a man they didn't know.

The following morning, gossip was rampant until an explanation came via one of the maids from the Worsley estate whose mother lived in the village. Sir Laurence had tipped over the curricle they'd all seen him and Miss Lyla in the day before. He'd been knocked unconscious. Miss Worsley had been rolled into a hedge, her bonnet had been ruined and she was bruised, but she had been able to go for help. Luckily, Mr. Gallagher, a visitor to her father from Ireland, had been out getting to know the neighborhood and had found her. They had returned to the scene of the accident but found the curricle and Sir Laurence gone. They guessed he'd somehow made his way home.

"Her poor bonnet!" said the maid. "You should have seen it, Mam. Totally ruined it were! And it come from Lunnon!"

The story was confirmed later in the day by a groom from the Breckenridge estate bringing in a horse to be shod. Sir Laurence had come to and had been able to right the curricle, but then he had swooned again and the horses had carried him home. In a terrible state, he was. His knee all banged up, two black eyes and a broken tooth. He'd taken to his bed and the doctor was attending him.

Chapter Forty-Six

The whole village turned out for the wedding of Finn Gallagher and Lyla Worsley. Sir Laurence's absence was explained by his still being under medical care, but the family sent a huge bouquet of flowers, which everyone agreed was very handsome. By that time Finn was known to all of them and everyone agreed it was no surprise dear Miss Worsley had fallen in love while she was in Ireland. The women considered him the most charming man and the men thought him a bang-up fellow. Harry Blankley agreed to be his groomsman. Potter was Lyla's bridesmaid, an unheard-of choice. There was a good deal of scandalized muttering about that, and Potter herself was hard to persuade.

"It's not fitting, Miss Lyla," she said. "You should have someone of your own rank."

"But you are my dearest friend! I could not have managed without you all these years, and especially not in Newbridge! I shall be very hurt if you don't accept, Potter, dear. Please say yes!"

So in the end, Potter came out of the church holding the train of the girl she had been like a mother to most of her life.

Lyla had never met any of Finn's family and was understandably anxious. But her worries proved unfounded. They proved as charming as their younger son. His older brother, a shorter and rounder version of Finn, with the same bright blue eyes, shook her hand heartily and said he was glad his tearaway younger brother had found a woman to take him in hand. His mother, a comfortable, white-haired lady, took her aside.

"The Lord be praised!" she said. "We were in despair of our Finn finding a wife, so we were. But anyone can see he loves you, and sure 'tis no wonder, as pretty and clever as you are. Thank you, my dear."

The couple agreed they would make their home principally in Middlesex, where Finn took over more and more of Lyla's father's functions. They went as often as they could to Ireland and specially to Newbridge, which always felt like a second home.

Jeb became a man of substance in the area and father to a large family of red-headed boys who tumbled around in the yard like puppies. He was ruled with an iron fist by his diminutive wife, and they were all ruled by Rascal and Scamp and their numerous offspring.

Eamon-John never went back to live in Ireland and it was many years before he even dared visit. He married his girl from the Breckenridge estate and worked his way up the Worsley stables until he became head groom. Miss Potter was Godmother to his children and was surrounded by people who loved her till the day she died.

Sir Laurence was hardly ever seen in the area, and when he was, he walked with a distinct limp. He claimed it was from his injuries when the curricle overturned. The good news as far as Lyla was concerned was that it prevented him from riding.

"Thank God," she said. "He always had a terrible seat."

The End

A Note from the Author

If you enjoyed this novel, please leave a review! Go to the Amazon page and scroll down past all the other books Amazon wants you to buy(!) till you get to the review click. It really does help independent authors like me. Thank you so much!

Click Here for the book page

Or use the QR code:

For a free short story, to listen to the first chapter of all my novels, and **for a token for a free audiobook**, please go to my website:

https://romancenovelsbyglrobinson.com

An excerpt from GL Robinson's next novel

I Have Always Loved You

A Second Chance Regency Romance

Let me say at once: I've never been good-looking. Perhaps if I'd had a mother to fuss over me and put my hair in curling papers or pat Denmark Lotion (I believe that's what it's called) on my skin, things might have been better, but honestly, I doubt it. You can't, as they say, make a silk purse out of a sow's ear.

Please don't think I'm looking for sympathy — I'm not. My Mama didn't die or anything dramatic like that. She went off with the man who was teaching her to paint watercolors. I don't know if she was particularly talented at this art form. We have no examples of it. She was probably too busy falling in love to actually do any painting.

I don't remember missing her very much, in fact I don't remember her at all. I once asked my father whether he missed her and he looked at me vaguely. "Who?" he said. And that answered the question. In fact, I don't suppose he realized for quite some time that she was gone. He would disappear into his laboratory with his chemistry experiments and not be seen for days. I daresay that's what caused my mother to prefer the artist. It doesn't take long to paint something with watercolors, and you don't need a laboratory to do it. In fact, one may watch while one's partner dashes one off. Or even be the subject of the oeuvre oneself: I've sometimes imagined my mother being painted by the adoring artist, lounging languidly on a chaise dressed in floating veils. I quite like that vision.

A man who prefers sodium chloride to oneself is not good husband material, and not much better as a father. I've always thought it amazing I was conceived at all. Perhaps my father had had a particularly spectacular result with a new reagent one day and grasped my mother around the waist in a joyful dance. Then one thing led to another, which was me. It's a nice idea, at any rate.

I hope you noticed my casual reference to *sodium chloride* and were impressed. How can a lady know such things, I hear you ask. In fact, that's just the scientific word for common household salt. I know a lot more fine-sounding words than that, and what the use or effects of the compounds concerned are. My father, not having a wife (at least, not one he could find around the house), taught me everything he knew. I can't say I was especially interested or a good student, but if it's a choice between sitting alone for days or being with your father while he pours stuff in and out of test tubes, you would probably end up listening, as I did. In the end, it was a good thing I did, as you will see.

My aunt (my father's sister) usually visited us about once a year and threatened to remove me from her careless brother's home. I suppose she thought that if he'd lost a wife, he might just as easily lose a daughter. But either because he didn't want to be the man pointed at as having lost two women in a row, or because he quite liked me, my father steadfastly refused to relinquish me. So I stayed with him and learned to read and write and to do sums by having him thrust his notes at me, telling me to copy them over, and by pulling any books I fancied (and could reach) from the dusty shelves in the library.

We had a maid of all work and a cook, and they taught me a lot too. Millie the maid showed me how to make a fire, wash the linen and iron without scorching the garment. I used to watch Cook the same as I watched my father. I learned what happened when you crumbled butter and flour in your fingers until it became a ball that you could flatten out with a rolling pin and fill with all sorts of stuff. I learned that you have to scald a chicken in boiling water for a few minutes to make the feathers come out easily. I learned that if you take the leftover bones from any meat and simmer them with onion and carrots you can make a sustaining broth. All of this went along with learning why metal and water produce oxidation (rusting) or proving that both combustion and breathing need oxygen (if you put a caged rat in a tightly closed box with a lit candle and open it up some time later you will find an extinguished candle and a dead rat — I know, I tried it.)

My aunt, on her infrequent visits, cried out in dismay at what she called my lack of education. By that, she meant I didn't know how to sketch or paint (the knowledge of my mother's disappearance had always put me off that pastime), or embroider, or cover a screen (why anyone would do so I couldn't imagine, didn't screens come with covers? If they didn't, they could hardly perform their function). I couldn't speak French or Italian and I couldn't play the pianoforte that hulked in the corner of the salon, untouched by anyone except the cat who liked to sleep on it in just the spot where the sun hit it in the afternoons. But, you know, I now think my very unusual education is just what all girls should have. Knowing how to launder, iron and cook and understand the elements of chemistry was much more useful in my life than tunelessly plonking out a sentimental ballad on the pianoforte or forcing visitors to admire my painting of unevenly risen loaves of bread that were supposed to be the Alps. I know it served me well in later life.

To pre-order *I Will Always Love You*, please go to:

https://www.amazon.com/dp/B0CQKPKQVM/

To find out more about my other Regency novels and short stories, please go to my Amazon author page:

https://www.amazon.com/stores/GL-Robinson/author/B08113Q84K

or to my website:

https://romancenovelsbyglrobinson.com

Thank you and happy reading!

About The Author

GL Robinson is a retired French professor who began writing Regency Romances in 2018. She dedicates all her books to her sister, who died unexpectedly that year and who, like her, had a lifelong love of the genre. She remembers the two of them reading Georgette Heyer after lights out under the covers in their convent boarding school and giggling together in delicious complicity.

Brought up in the south of England, she has spent the last forty years in upstate New York with her American husband. She likes gardening, talking with her grandchildren and sitting by the fire with a good book and a nice cup of tea! She still reads Georgette Heyer.

Printed in Great Britain
by Amazon